A MOONLIGHT MEETING

Until her wonderful chance encounter with handsome Tom Fallon, Megan's future had been all arranged. When her childhood sweetheart, Larry, had a job which could support two, it came almost too late. For Megan seemed to have fallen under Tom's spell and was no longer sure if she would be happy as Larry's wife. And it was only in the aftermath of a terrible tragedy that Megan realized the true meaning of love . . .

PEGGY GADDIS

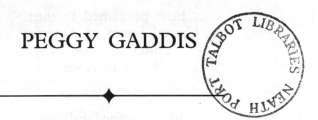

A MOONLIGHT MEETING

Complete and Unabridged

LINFORD
Leicester

First published in the
United States of America
under the title of
'Frost in April'

First Linford Edition
published 1997

British Library CIP Data

Gaddis, Peggy
    A moonlight meeting.—Large print ed.—
Linford romance library
    1. American fiction—20th century
    2. Large type books
    I. Title
    813.5'2 [F]

    ISBN 0–7089–5035–3

Published by
F. A. Thorpe (Publishing) Ltd.
Anstey, Leicestershire

Set by Words & Graphics Ltd.
Anstey, Leicestershire
Printed and bound in Great Britain by
T. J. International Ltd., Padstow, Cornwall

This book is printed on acid-free paper

1

MEGAN MacTAVISH finished writing checks for the month's bills, and straightened, wearily. There were six cows to be milked, and Amos, the hired hand, was so slow that unless Megan milked three of them herself it would be dark before the job was finished. For perhaps the one thousandth time since her mother's death, she wished her father would take over some of the responsibilities of running their small Georgia farm.

As she went out of the small sitting room that was her 'office' she glanced across the road and saw the glimmer of lights in the little cottage that was her nearest neighbor. So Alicia Stevenson had returned from her visit to Atlanta. She knew a moment of sharp envy for Alicia's ease and freedom from the gruelling farm labor that was the lot of practically all the residents of Pleasant Grove. Busy with milking, a task which she had done so many times that it was purely automatic, she found herself thinking about Alicia.

Late one June evening, the New York Limited, which ordinarily raced through Pleasant Grove with merely a derisive toot of its lordly whistle, had stopped and a woman had alighted, a woman of perhaps forty, smartly dressed according to Pleasant Grove standards, and surrounded by a sea of luggage. She had announced herself, in Burns Mercantile, Pleasant Grove's general store, as Alicia Stevenson, and stated that she had come to live in the old Brigham place.

From the very first, Alicia had made it plain that she loathed Pleasant Grove. She loved cities, and she hated being buried in the country. But with equal frankness she admitted that the small income on which she lived had shrunk until it was no longer possible for her to live in a city, and so she had come to Pleasant Grove.

Megan finished the milking, and she and Amos took the brimming milk pails to the spring house, cool and dark, where the milk would be left overnight and where, in the morning, Annie, Amos' wife, would churn.

Coming back across the backyard, almost completely dark now that the sun had gone and twilight was deepening, she saw a man standing waiting for her at the steps and was startled. He was a stranger, and strangers — specially masculine strangers — were sufficiently rare in Pleasant Grove to arouse a bit of surprise.

"Miss MacTavish?" He came towards her, smiling, and she saw that he was tall and rugged looking and that he must have been close to forty. "I'm Tom Fallon — your neighbor down the road there. We've just moved in, and they told me that you might be willing to supply us with milk and butter and eggs."

"Why, yes, I think so," said Megan,

and then remembered. "Oh, you're the new High School principal! Welcome to Pleasant Grove!"

"Thank you," said Tom, and his handshake was warm and friendly. "That's very kind of you."

"It's going to be nice to have someone in the Westbrook place," said Megan pleasantly. "I'd like to call on Mrs Fallon as soon as you are settled."

She saw the shadow fall over his face. Even in the dusk she could sense the tightening, the stiffening, that made him look suddenly older and somehow, aloof.

"You're very kind," he told her formally. "But Mrs Fallon is — an invalid. Her health does not permit her to have callers. Her sister lives with us and takes care of her."

"Oh — I'm sorry," said Megan quickly, and meant it. "You will let us know, though, if there is anything we can do to help? We pride ourselves on being neighborly in Pleasant Grove."

4

Tom smiled and the darkening of his face was gone now. He said pleasantly, "I'd almost forgot that such a thing existed — neighborliness, I mean. You don't find any evidences of it in a city any more."

"I suppose you would like some supplies tonight, if you're just getting in?" suggested Megan, leading the way into the kitchen.

And while she and Tom chatted politely and pleasantly, she got out an old-fashioned sweet-grass basket, put a clean napkin in the bottom of it, counted out a dozen eggs from the big yellow bowl on the refrigerator, added a pound of fresh butter, a jar of preserves, and a loaf of Annie's freshly baked bread, and cut a thick, generous slice from the big ham that hung, neatly wrapped, in the pantry.

"How much?" said Tom, when he had thanked her and accepted the basket.

"Why, nothing at all," she told him, surprised that he should ask such a question. "That's merely a welcoming basket — nobody in Pleasant Grove would charge for that!"

"Oh, see here, now — " Tom protested and Megan laughed.

"Beginning tomorrow, you can pay for your milk and butter and eggs," she assured him lightly. "But for tonight — there is no charge. It's the custom here."

Tom looked down at the well-laden basket and then at Megan, and she saw that his eyes were warmly blue and that he looked touched and pleased, as well as surprised.

"Well — thanks, of course — I'm a little too surprised to know what else to say," he told her frankly. "I believe I'm going to like Pleasant Grove a lot."

"We all hope so," she answered him, smiling.

2

THERE was something about Tom Fallon that made Megan feel sorry for him; something, too, that put her on the defensive when he and his family affairs were being discussed. Pleasant Grove was a small town where everybody knew everybody else's business.

She liked Tom Fallon; and she had called at the old Westbrook place in the friendly, neighborly fashion and taken with her small delicacies calculated to tempt the appetite of an invalid. But she had never gone beyond the front porch. Here she had always been met by the 'big, husky-lookin'' woman who was Martha Evans. She was always polite, yet extremely brief; offerings for the invalid were accepted with a minimum of thanks and an entire lack of any evidence of a willingness to be sociable. Yet Megan refused to see in this anything but an entirely laudable desire to protect an invalid who was unable to cope with visitors.

Besides, Megan told herself dryly as she went busily about her days, she had little time to try to thrust herself on people who were quite satisfied without her presence; but she resented her friends' and neighbors' prying curiosity and endless wondering about Tom Fallon and his family affairs.

Megan's favorite relaxation, when she could find time for it, was a walk to the top of the low-lying hill beyond the meadow that rejoiced in the ambitious title of the Ridge. Annie used to laugh delightedly at the sight of Megan setting out for her walk, on the afternoons when she was free for such activity. Megan's steps towards the barn were a signal of her intention, and brought the two dogs leaping and barking joyously about her; behind the dogs came the four cats. Beyond the cats came such of the chickens as had managed to make their escape from the chicken yard, and then as Megan and her 'entourage' crossed the meadow, Midgie, the smallest of the Jersey cows, usually elected to go to walk, too; and if there was a calf, as there usually was, it went also.

On an afternoon late in October, Megan emerged from the barbed wire fence and straightened, to look back down the low meadow valley. The dogs were scampering wildly; Dixie, the small black water spaniel who was a superb hunter self-taught, had treed game and was barking his head off; Bessie, the pointer, was racing through the underbrush at the edge of the pines, her tail quivering with delight at the scent she had disturbed; while the cats were climbing trees with joyous abandon.

"The whole thing takes on the aspect of a three-ring circus," Megan told herself, laughing a little as she turned and went on up the Ridge, to the top where her favorite flat stone would be waiting for her to rest on its smooth surface.

But as she stepped out of the pines to the small clearing where the rock lay, she paused and said, startled, "Oh — I'm sorry — I didn't know there was anyone here."

Tom stood up, smiling, eager.

"Well, Miss MacTavish! How are you? Am I trespassing on your property?" he said quickly.

"Oh, no, as a matter of fact this property belongs to your place," Megan assured him. "The circus and I just use it as a finish to our walk."

"Shall I go?" suggested Tom lightly.

"Of course not — how silly," protested Megan swiftly; "After all, there are two rocks and plenty of room for both of us!"

"Thanks," said Tom, and smiled as he watched her settle herself on the rock while he selected another one.

Megan said, after a moment, "How is Mrs. Fallon? Does the climate seem to agree with her, as you'd hoped?"

Tom's brown hand tightened about the bowl of his pipe until the knuckles stood up in little white mounds. He tore his eyes from the landscape and gave her a look that was hard and cold and bitter, so much so that she was startled by the sudden, inexplicable hostility.

"Mrs. Fallon is — doing as well as could be expected, under the circumstances," he told her. His voice was harsh, and the very sound of the words told her that he had repeated these words until they had ceased to have any meaning; yet he had never ceased to resent the necessity for them.

"I'm sorry if I seemed — inquisitive or rude," Megan told him frankly, her face hot with color, her head up. "I had no such intention. You have made no secret of the fact that your wife is an invalid. Naturally, in a small town like this, people are interested and anxious to be of service, if they may — "

"The only service anyone can do my

wife — or myself — is to leave my wife alone," stated Tom, and Megan's eyes blazed at his tone.

She was on her feet now, and she said swiftly, her voice shaking with anger, "You may be quite sure that in the future, I, at least, shall be happy to do so!"

She turned blindly to walk back through the pines, but before she had gone half a dozen steps, Tom was on his feet, laying a hand on her arm, in swift, abject apology.

"Please wait — please, forgive me," he apologized humbly. "That was unforgivable of me! It's just that — well, the subject is — an extremely painful one — "

"I'm sincerely sorry that I mentioned it," she told him stiffly, her face still hot.

He looked down at her gravely, his hand still on her arm, restraining her as she would have walked away.

"You see, Miss MacTavish," he said at last, his voice raw with pain, "my wife's illness is — chiefly mental."

He set his teeth hard when he had spoken the last two words, and Megan looked up at him, puzzled.

"Mental? You mean she merely imagines she is ill? That she is a hypochondriac?" she asked, in all innocence.

Tom's face was white and rigid now, but his eyes were alive with pain.

"No," he said huskily. "I mean that my wife is — mentally ill — that she has the mind of a young child — that she is not — not normal!"

It was obvious that he had tried to say 'insane' and had not been able to get the word past his stiff lips.

Megan was conscious of a moment of stunned, shocked horror. *"Oh!"* was all she could say, her tone shocked and rich with sympathy and touched with keen embarrassment that she must witness his moment of naked, burning revelation. "I'm — terribly sorry — "

Tom brushed aside the choked, inadequate words and said with a sort of forced quiet, "So you see why it has been necessary for us to — deny the well intentioned callers — "

"Of course," Megan told him unsteadily, sick with pity for him.

"She is — entirely harmless," he told her, and his face was wrenched with the pain and the shame of having to put that thought into words. "She is never left for a moment alone and she never leaves her bed. But if people here knew about her — mental condition — well, undoubtedly they would — well, feel that she should be locked away! Put in an institution — " The pain of the thought silenced his words for a moment, and after he had got himself somewhat under control he managed a smile at her that was little more than a grimace and said, "So now you know. What are you going to do?"

Megan's face flamed with hurt.

"You may be quite sure that I shall reveal your secret to no one — why should I? What right — or necessity — would I have?" she told him sharply.

Tom smiled at her, a white, faint smile that was somehow very tragic.

"I know you wouldn't. Forgive me. I'm clumsy and stupid, but not intentionally or willfully so. Forgive me — for everything?"

Megan melted beneath the look in his eyes, and put her hand in his and let him draw her back to the flat stone, where she sat down once more. And as though the revelation of his tragic secret had cleared the air between them, as though they were friends now, they spoke of other things.

His mind was keen and alert; Megan read a great deal and used her mind to think with, and it was for both of them a pleasant experience to be able to talk of things that had nothing to do with Pleasant Grove. Megan liked her friends and her neighbors, but there were many times when she hungered for impersonal talk of matters far afield from Pleasant Grove, and she enjoyed this contact with a stimulating mind.

He walked with her to the barbed

wire fence, when she saw that she must go because the evening was ending; he laughed a little, and obligingly held up the lower strand of barbed wire so she could crawl under it without snagging her crisp gingham dress.

"There really should be a gate here," she told him, getting to her feet on the other side of the fence, laughing across the four strands of barbed wire at him. "But I'm like the man who was going to fix the leak in his roof, only he couldn't work while it was raining; and when it wasn't raining the roof didn't need mending. I somehow never get around to it!"

She whistled. The two dogs came bounding to her, and the four cats stepped daintily out of a great thicket of honeysuckle vines that sprawled at the corner of the fence. And as she walked back down the meadow path to the brook, she looked over her shoulder, and lifted her hand to him in a gay little gesture, as she saw him still standing there. He lifted his hat to her and bowed in a gay burlesque of a sweeping old-world gesture, and she went on, her heart a little lighter for him. She was terribly sorry for him, but she admired the gallantry with which he carried his burdens. And, looking across the fields towards the drab little five-room frame house that was the Westbrook place and that now held this pathetic woman, his wife, she felt the tears in her eyes. Poor man! and — poor woman! She shivered a little and hurried as she went, as though to run away from thoughts that bit too deeply.

3

ONE of Pleasant Grove's favorite Autumn diversions was quilting parties. Through the scant leisure time of winter, most of Pleasant Grove's women pieced quilts, out of 'scrap bags' and carefully hoarded bits of material; and then when the quilt top had been pieced and finished, the owner notified her friends that she was 'putting up' a quilt and they were invited to come and help her quilt it.

The quilt frame, an oblong composed of four strips of narrow, carefully planed and splinterless wood, held together at the corners by pegs, would be swung from hooks in the ceiling and held stationary at a level comfortable for women seated about it. The quilt top, the smooth roll of cotton batting, and the lining, already basted together, would be tacked between the four narrow strips, held taut, and the women gathered about would take small, dainty, firm stitches, either following the pattern of the pieces in the quilt, or a semicircle of their own selection and arrangement.

A few days after her talk with Tom on the Ridge, Megan went over to Mrs. Stuart's, where there was a quilting. Megan had not been able to go for the whole day, as most of the women had, each bringing a dish of her own concocting to add to the midday dinner which would be served at twelve o'clock; she went in the afternoon, to have a part in the second quilt of the day. The morning's product, a 'Step-Around-the-Mountain' pattern, was spread on the bed in Mrs. Stuart's 'comp'ny bedroom' and Megan paused to admire it before going on in the 'settin' room,' where the frame had already been set up with the second quilt, a 'Rose of Sharon' pattern.

There were greetings, a breezy exchange of pleasantries, while Megan settled herself, brought her thimble out of her pocket, threaded her needle, and set to work.

There were perhaps a dozen women about the big frame, which was opened to its fullest width, the width and length of a double bed.

Suddenly, Megan heard the name, "'fessor Fallon" and looked up. Across the quilt frame from her, Alicia Stevenson was watching her shrewdly, a little knowing look in her small, dark eyes that made Megan oddly and absurdly uneasy.

Mrs. Burns, who was president of the Parent-Teachers' Association of the local school, was saying, "I think we're lucky to get a man like Professor Fallon here. The School Board says his qualifications are excellent and his references are extremely good!"

"Maybe Megan could tell us more about him than that," said Alicia silkily.

"About what?" asked Megan, cravenly pretending not to understand.

"Why a man like Tom Fallon would be satisfied in a little hick town like Pleasant Grove," said Alicia, smiling. "After all, you know him so much better than any of the rest of us — "

"I sell him milk and butter and eggs, yes," Megan told her curtly. "I'd hardly say that made us old friends, though."

"But I thought during some of those long hours you've spent together on the Ridge, he might have told you something of himself," suggested Alicia, limpid-eyed, her voice soft as satin.

There was a startled gasp about the quilting frame, perhaps not so much a gasp as a sense of movement that made Megan know they were all staring at her, startled, wondering — waiting.

Megan drew a long breath. "Just what do you mean by that?" she asked Alicia sharply.

Alicia's eyes were wide with surprise, but there was a trace of malice in their depths also.

"But, *darling*," she protested, her

voice artificially gay and sweet, "what could I *possibly* mean except that I've seen you and the gallant professor on the Ridge — "

"Once, quite by accident, when I was out for a walk — " Megan began, but Alicia interrupted her with pretty concern and an apology that was worse than the most open accusation.

"Of course, I'm terribly sorry," Alicia interrupted. "Please don't say any more. I never dreamed — I mean I wouldn't have mentioned it for the world — " She was prettily confused, and Megan could feel the hint of tension, of curiosity, that crept about the room.

The women who had been her friends and neighbors all her life looked at her and then quickly away, very carefully not meeting her eyes, trying not to meet each other's eyes, elaborately pretending to be very casual.

"This is ridiculous!" said Megan hotly. "You're trying to make people believe that I've been — sneaking off to meet Mr. Fallon — "

Megan was trembling a little, though she knew she was being silly. The little scene with Tom Fallon had been so absurdly innocent; yet there was something in the sly, furtive manner of Alicia's mentioning it that had made it seem evil and scheming.

She looked swiftly around the group that bent above the Rose of Sharon quilt. Everybody was intent on the job; nobody looked up or met her eyes; and after a tense moment, Mrs. Stuart said something casual to her neighbor, and the neighbor answered her with such obvious relief that little spatters of meaningless conversation swept up about the scene and Megan's encounter with Alicia was apparently forgotten.

But Megan, taking clumsy stitches in her part of the quilt, felt anger seethe through her; anger and a slight twinge of uneasiness. After all, everybody knew what Alicia was like. But Megan knew that the little town held rather rigid views regarding the conduct of the teachers to whom their children were entrusted, and she tried to tell herself that she was being silly to let Alicia get under her skin; but any unpleasant gossip, stemming from even so slight a thing as this, could have unpleasant repercussions, so far as Tom Fallon was concerned. Remembering his white, tortured face and his eyes, as he had revealed to her the pitiful secret of his wife's mental condition, she had a moment of sick apprehension for the future.

4

FOR the next two or three days, although she told herself she was being a fool, Megan deliberately avoided seeing Tom Fallon at all. He had been in the habit of stopping on his way home from school late in the afternoon to get the milk, butter, and eggs which he bought from her. She had always been the one to give them to him, but for the next two or three days, she saw to it that she was somewhere else when he stopped by, and Annie, puzzled and watchful, waited on him.

But on Saturday, she was in the chicken yard checking up on a setting hen who was due to hatch her brood in a few days, when Tom came to the back fence and spoke to her.

"Good morning," he said, almost warily.

Megan turned, startled, and felt her face grow hot, even as she greeted him casually and matter-of-factly.

He waited for her to come to the fence before he said anxiously, "I've been a little worried — and deeply puzzled. I've tried my darndest to think what I could have done to upset you — "

Megan looked up at him and said quietly, and frankly, "I see you haven't heard the news, Mr. Fallon!"

Puzzled, noting her use of the formal prefix rather than the careless friendly 'Professor' that was almost a nickname, he said quickly, "News? No, I'm afraid I haven't — "

"I feel very silly to be relaying it to you — but I know Pleasant Grove so well — the attitude towards teachers, especially towards the principal of the school — " She floundered miserably and was silent.

Tom said quietly, "I think you had better tell me straight, Miss MacTavish."

"There seems to be a rumor about that you and I have been meeting secretly on the Ridge." She let him have it almost in a single breath.

Tom stared at her as though he thought she had lost her mind. And then his face hardened and his eyes blazed and he said through his teeth, "Where in blazes — who'd try to start a lie like that?"

Megan made a weary little gesture.

"It's too silly, and too — cheap to notice," she pointed out to him. "Except that since you are new here and this is your first year — oh, I feel an utter fool about the whole thing. But I thought it would be better if we — well, we've done nothing to *start* gossip, so it seems a little difficult to know how to stop it — "

Tom said sternly, "Who started this talk?"

"Mrs. Stevenson," answered Megan frankly. "She happened to be on the Ridge the afternoon we met by accident, and chose to believe that we

27

were meeting there regularly — and as secretly as possible — "

"But that's nonsense — she couldn't possibly believe anything so — so — damned silly!" Tom exploded.

"I don't think she really believes it, but she seems to get quite a lot of pleasure out of dropping little significant remarks — innuendos that are so hard to counteract — " Megan broke down helplessly and spread her hands in a gesture of futility. "So there you have it."

Puzzled, Tom said, "Who is this Mrs. Stevenson?"

Megan shook her head. "She is a widow. She came here to live in the spring, because, as she frankly stated, her income is so small she can't afford to live anywhere else. And she amuses herself by ferreting out small things that people would rather not have known — and then — sort of broadcasts them where they will create the most excitement."

"She sounds like a thoroughly

unpleasant person," said Tom grimly. "And a dangerous one.

"You don't think, by any chance, that she — overheard our conversation that day?" Tom suggested, and the shadow in his eyes was so deep that Megan felt a wrench of pity.

"I'm quite sure she didn't," she answered him honestly and swiftly. "Because if she had, she would have — broadcast long before this."

Tom said sternly, suddenly, "I think I'll have a little talk with Mrs. Stevenson."

But Megan laid a swift hand on his arm, stopping him.

"Please don't," she said urgently. "After all, nothing can be gained by talking to her. We've all tried it — she only uses our protests and arguments to add more fuel to her talk. We've found that the best way is to avoid her, and give her as little material as we can."

"But the woman's a menace — " protested Tom angrily. He broke off to look at her curiously, frowning in angry amazement. "See here — you're not afraid of her?"

Megan managed a confused, unhappy laugh.

"I'm afraid we all are — a little," she admitted frankly. "After all, these little — well, stories that she drops about here and there can make things — well, difficult and not too pleasant. But we all try to ignore her."

Tom nodded grimly. "Just the same, I think I'll have a little talk with her," he said, and before Megan could stop him he had turned and strode away in the direction of the little silvery-gray house with its green trim.

She watched him until the trees enclosing the house had swallowed him up and then she finished her work in the chicken yard and went back across the hard-packed back yard to the house. She was uneasy, and angry. The whole situation was so completely without reason. Why had she not merely laughed at Alicia's little innuendo and let it drop? But even as the thought crossed her mind, she knew that she could not have done it; that the suddenly guarded faces about her, the wary eyes that slipped expressionlessly away from hers, had made it impossible for her to do anything but protest the insinuation Alicia's light, carefully sweet voice had dropped with such apparent innocence but such very real malicious enjoyment.

It was almost half an hour before Tom came back and stopped at the back door to get the two bottles of milk and the eggs that she had waiting for him.

His face was grim and set. There was a little white line about his mouth, and his eyes were angry. But he managed a slight smile that tried hard to be comforting, and said quietly, "I don't think you need to worry any more. And there is no reason why you should not continue your walks to the Ridge, any time you like. I think Mrs. Stevenson is going to mend her ways a bit."

"Thanks," said Megan, trying to

pretend that she felt relieved. "I hope so."

He picked up the milk and the sack of eggs and went his way.

Megan stood still for a moment. She could almost feel pity for Alicia; for any woman who had come to a small, friendly, peaceful town like Pleasant Grove and who had, in the brief space of a few months completely destroyed all the friendliness towards herself, and who had surrounded herself with so much hate and ill will was, to Megan, pathetic. But remembering the look of malicious enjoyment on Alicia's face that afternoon when she had flung that outrageous if oblique charge at Megan, her feeling of pity vanished. It was only too plain that Alicia enjoyed setting people by the ears; she seemed to get a kick out of knowing that people resented and feared her.

Megan shook off her unhappy thoughts, as Annie announced that supper was ready. She and her father sat down in the dining room, and her father began giving her a brisk account of his day, which had apparently consisted chiefly of airing his superior knowledge of world affairs to such of his cronies as he could find at Will Arnold's Service Station, which was Pleasant Grove's equivalent to a club.

They were not more than halfway through supper when the front door opened and a cheerful voice called, "Yoo-hoo — it's only me! I'll just come right in."

It was Alicia, of course, cool and fresh looking in a brown and yellow print frock, her hair brushed into coquettish curls, a yellow bow tucked into it. She was rather heavily rouged as usual, and if she was feeling the unpleasantness of Tom's visit, she certainly did not show it.

Jim MacTavish, always with an eye for an attractive woman, greeted her with obvious pleasure, and drew out a chair for her. She demurred prettily at their invitation to have supper, but was persuaded to have just a bit of the baked spareribs, just a bit of the homemade sauerkraut, one of Annie's hot biscuits — until she had managed to consume a substantial meal. And then she broached the object of her visit; she had bought some new window shades for her house and was completely helpless when it came to putting them up, and wondered — so prettily! — if Mr. MacTavish would give her a hand.

Jim expressed himself as delighted to be of service, as he rose from the table and went to get his tools. Alicia turned to Megan and said softly, limpid-eyed, "I'm terribly sorry that you and Mr. Fallon were so upset at my seeing you on the Ridge, darling. Why in the world didn't you tell me it was a secret? I should have been terribly discreet if I'd only known — "

Megan said harshly, "There was nothing in the least secret about it, Alicia, as I tried to tell you. It was purely an accident, and of no more importance than if we had met on the public street in front of the Mercantile."

Alicia said sadly, "You're angry with me, Megan. I'm terribly sorry. I wouldn't upset you for the world."

Megan said curtly, "Let's skip it, shall we?"

Alicia hesitated and then she lifted her thin shoulders in a little shrug and said, "Of course — why not?"

A moment later she and Jim were going down the steps and along the walk.

Megan went on into the shabby, comfortable living room and sat down with a mending basket. But though she sewed until after ten, which was disgracefully late according to Pleasant Grove's early-to-bed, early-to-rise habits, her father had not come home when she finally went to bed. Indeed, she had been in bed for some time and was almost asleep before she heard his cautious entrance and the door of his room closing behind him.

In the morning, she had already had

her breakfast and done her morning chores before her father came down. He was at the table, having his final cup of coffee, when she came into the dining room. He looked up at her a little defensively.

"That Mrs. Stevenson is a delightful little woman," he stated firmly. "I can't think what this filthy-minded little town means by low-rating her as they have. I've heard all sorts of gossip about her. I have never had a chance to get acquainted with her — but now that I have, I intend to defend her whenever I get a chance."

Megan looked at him, startled, and then she smiled.

"Okay, Galahad," she told him teasingly. "But you're mapping out a busy winter for yourself."

"It's outrageous for people to talk about a defenseless woman — " began Jim truculently.

Megan put her hands on the back of one of the old-fashioned chairs, and leaned towards him.

"Look, Pops," she said firmly, "Alicia is getting exactly the treatment she seems to want. She has an absolutely scandalous tongue and she goes around making people miserable by ferreting out their pitiful little secrets and broadcasting them — "

"Are you accusing her of being a liar?" demanded her father sharply.

Megan hesitated, and then shrugged. "Well, perhaps not entirely," she admitted. "There is usually some small grain of truth in what she says, and the rest is inference."

"People have no right to be upset about the truth — " her father began sternly.

Megan said quietly, "At Mrs. Stuart's quilting, she dropped the information that I have been seen meeting Professor Fallon secretly on the Ridge."

Jim stared at her for a moment, and then his handsome, ruddy face began to darken with anger. "Is that true, Megan?" he demanded sternly.

"I met him on the Ridge once,

purely by accident, and talked to him a few minutes," Megan answered quietly. "After all, he is a customer of ours — he is a fine, intelligent, interesting man. I couldn't very well turn around and walk away, refusing to speak to him, could I?"

"Certainly not — but you didn't have to keep going back to meet him again," snapped Jim furiously.

Megan held on to her temper with an effort.

"I've just told you that I saw him there just once, purely by accident," she told him levelly.

"Well, then, what's all the fuss about?" snapped Jim.

"The fuss is because Alicia gave the impression at Mrs Stuart's that I was meeting Tom there almost daily — and in secret," Megan returned.

"Then you should have explained — "

"I did," Megan cut in. "But — the harm had already been done."

"Harm? What possible harm could come from such a thing?"

"None at all, except that Alicia dropped her little information in the exact way to make it sound ugliest — and of course the women around the quilting frame were most of them mothers with children in the school, and they promptly began to wonder — you could almost see them wondering — just how much truth there was in the suggestion, and whether Tom was the right man to hold the job he's got — "

"You keep calling him 'Tom,'" her father cut in suddenly, and there was a curious, almost a suspicious look in his eyes.

Megan set her teeth for a moment, and then answered quietly, "I have never called him anything but 'Mr. Fallon' or 'Professor Fallon' to his face."

"Then it seems a bit odd you would speak of him as 'Tom' — as though you always thought of him as 'Tom,'" her father pointed out.

Megan made a gesture of helplessness.

"You see how well Alicia does her work?" she said dryly. "You wonder why the women at the quilting party yesterday afternoon could think for a moment there was any truth in what she was hinting — and yet you yourself, my own father, are wondering uneasily if maybe I haven't been just a little — well, indiscreet!"

Jim rose from the table and flung his crumpled napkin down and snorted.

"That's idiotic! I'm not wondering anything of the kind! Maybe Alicia Stevenson chatters too much — but I'm convinced it's merely a guilty conscience that makes people think she's talking maliciously. You know the old saying — 'if the shoe pinches' — " and he strode out of the house.

5

FOR the past two years, Megan had had two dates a week with Laurence Martin, who worked in the law office of old Judge Graham, at the county seat, getting much valuable experience and very little money. He and Megan had grown up together in Pleasant Grove, although Laurence was older than she by several years.

He came over on Thursday nights on the bus, arriving at Pleasant Grove at seven-fifteen, and leaving on the ten-twenty-five bus. He came again on Sundays, usually for Sunday dinner and the afternoon.

On this Thursday night, Megan dressed for his arrival, with a feeling of relief that she was not facing any complication in Laurence's arrival. She liked him sincerely. She had, she admitted to herself, thought of marrying him. He wanted her to, when, as, and if he ever achieved a position that would make it possible for him to support a wife. That was an understanding between them that had no need to be put into words.

Tonight, standing before the mirror in her neat, cheerful bedroom, she studied her reflection in the mirror, with a soberness and an intensity that she seldom bothered to give the girl in the glass. She seldom had time to do more than glance at herself as she brushed her hair; but tonight, dressed and ready for Laurence, she looked at herself thoughtfully trying to see herself with the eyes of someone else, of a stranger — perhaps of Tom Fallon.

She saw a girl of a little over medium height, a neat, trim, well-rounded figure born of the hard work and outdoor exercise of her daily life; she saw leaf-brown hair that she wore shoulder length; her eyes were her best feature, her chief claim to beauty. They were gray-blue, long-lashed, set well apart beneath airy brows. She was not beautiful, she told herself with an almost impersonal frankness. She looked healthy and wholesome, and that was all!

It was so seldom she had the time to stop and dispassionately consider her claim to good looks that for a moment she was almost abashed at her own thoughts. And then she shrugged, settled the folds of her soft yellow flannel dress about her and went downstairs.

As she reached the foot of the stairs her father turned almost guiltily, from the front door, and said stiffly, "I knew Laurence would be along soon so I thought I'd step out for a little fresh air."

He was dressed, she saw, in his 'best' suit, ordinarily reserved for trips to the county seat and rare trips to the city more than a hundred miles away. He was freshly shaven, immaculately groomed — and, she told herself, almost a little surprised, he was downright handsome. He looked less than his forty-nine years, holding himself erectly, as though in an effort to disclaim the threat of impending overweight.

"For a walk? At this time of night?" she protested, surprised.

"It's seven o'clock," her father told her almost curtly. He let himself out of the house and closed the door behind him with a finality that was an effective end to any attempt she might make at discovering the reason for his unprecedented nighttime exercise.

She went into the living room and tidied it a bit. The night was chilly enough to make the log fire not only picturesque but distinctly welcome. She straightened the magazines her father had flung down, picked up a few petals that had spilled from the bowl of late roses on a corner table, and drew the curtains.

Almost before she had finished there was the brisk ring of purposeful footsteps on the old bricked walk, and a moment later the outer door opened and Laurence came in, beaming as he saw her, greeting her eagerly. He shed his light topcoat and hung it with his hat in its accustomed corner of the closet beneath the stairs.

"That looks good." He greeted the open fire and stood before it, warming his hands. "It's a bit nippy out tonight, and darker than a pocket. I was glad of my pocket flash before I got here."

He stood on the hearth rug, smiling down at her, and she felt a rush of warmth that was almost — perhaps it was — affection for him. He was so good and kind and honest! He was her friend!

He stood, tall and bony, and a little stooped, as though his height had run away from his weight. His thick, dark hair was brushed neatly back from an intelligent forehead. His eyes were brown and steady behind the hornrimmed eye-glasses, his jaw was square and dogged, his mouth thin-lipped, rather generous but pleasant.

Suddenly he grinned at her, and said, "Well? Do you see anything different about me? Have I changed?"

Megan's eyebrows went up a little. "No — has something happened?"

"As a matter of fact, it has. But you were looking at me so intently — almost as though you'd never seen me before — that I wondered."

"I'm a little tired, I guess," she apologized.

"I don't doubt it," answered Laurence, his tone warm. "You do enough work for three women, and it's a darned shame. If your father would face up to his responsibilities — "

He broke off as he saw the slight stiffening of her manner. "Sorry — I had no right to say that, of course. But I can't keep from thinking."

"Let's not quarrel tonight," she suggested quickly.

"Of course not. Let's not quarrel — ever," said Laurence swiftly. He sat down beside her on the shabby, comfortable old lounge and putting out his hand, took hers and held it warmly, companionably. "I've got much more important things to discuss tonight I got quite a boost up today — I could hardly wait to get here and tell you about it."

"I'm glad. What is it?" Her interest was honest and eager.

"Well, the old Judge called me in this afternoon, and told me that he plans to retire next year," Laurence told her eagerly. "The old fellow's getting on and he's pretty tired. But he wants me to take over, beginning now, so that in a year he can slip gracefully out of the picture and I can carry on!"

"That's splendid, Larry — but no more than you deserve," Megan told him swiftly and eagerly.

He nodded, his eyes very steady and very serious behind his rimmed glasses. "Thanks, honey," he answered, and went on before she could take note of the endearment, "It affects you, too, of course. That is, I hope it does."

His smile was confident, assured.

Obviously he was so sure of her that his qualification of the statement had been merely a surface matter.

"Meggie, you must have known all along that as soon as I got to a point where I felt sure I could take care of you I wanted you to marry me," he went on quietly. "I've got to that point now, so — will you, Meggie?"

Megan hesitated before answering. Hesitated so long her eyes on the fire, her hand lax beneath his own, that Laurence looked at her in sudden sharp alarm, and said quickly, "Look here, lady — it's polite to speak when you're spoken to."

"I'm sorry, Larry." She turned to him in quick, contrite apology. "It's just that — well, I scarcely know what to say."

Laurence was surprised and a little dashed. But his hand closed more warmly over hers and he said with an effort at lightening the threatening tension, "Well, 'yes' would be nice."

"I wish — it could be 'yes,'" she

admitted frankly.

Laurence turned sharply, so that he was sitting sideways on the lounge, facing her squarely. His thick, dark brows were drawn together in a puzzled frown and his eyes were apprehensive.

"See here, Meggie, what are you giving me? You're not suddenly going all coy on me?" he demanded anxiously.

"Of course not." She tried hard to laugh at the idea, but it was not a convincing laugh.

"Of course, I didn't do it with the proper buildup," he admitted with a crooked grin.

"Don't be an idiot!" Megan was grateful for his lightness and tried to rise to it. "It's only that — well, you have taken me a little by surprise — "

"Oh, come, now, Meggie — not 'this is so sudden,'" he protested mockingly.

"I know — I do sound like a fool," she admitted quite honestly.

The raillery was gone from his voice and his eyes when he spoke again. His tone was quiet and steady, his eyes gentle and warm.

"You have known all along, Meggie, that I love you. I think it first started when we were kids. Every man has somewhere in his mind or his heart, or both, a picture of the ideal — and there's never for a moment been anyone but you in that place for me. Everything I've done, every thought I've had for the future, has had you all woven into it and through it. It's been pretty bad these last two or three years watching you struggle to hold on to things here and not being able to help you. But now — well, all that's changed, Meggie. I've got an income that is modest enough in all conscience, but it can take care of you now and it will grow. I'll take care of you, Meggie, and I promise it will be easier for you than it has been in the past. I'll see to that! So — will you let me, Meggie? Because I love you and because I can't visualize any kind of life without you."

There were tears in her eyes, and her heart gave a warm throb as she turned to him and said, "Yes, Larry — if you're sure you want me."

Laurence said huskily, "As if I could ever be as sure of anything else in my life!"

He took her into his arms, awkwardly, as though she had been something so infinitely fragile and precious that the slightest careless touch might destroy her; yet there was a strength and an urgent tenderness in his touch that made her heart stir unaccustomedly.

There were so many things to be considered, so many problems to be settled. But tonight was no time for them. Tonight it was enough just to know one's self deeply beloved; to know that she was first in Laurence's thoughts, as she had been for a long, long time.

When he left, with fifteen minutes to catch his bus she went slowly up the stairs to her own room and sat for a while in the darkness, lit by the silver square of Autumn moonlight that spilled through the window. She was ashamed of herself that she should feel, not the exultant, delirious happiness of a girl newly engaged, but only a weariness that seemed to drug her limbs and to slow her heart.

The high, ecstatic thrills that were supposed to flood a girl's heart at a moment like this, seemed to have passed her by. She loved Laurence, of course; she assured herself of that again, ever more firmly, and was a little alarmed at the necessity of such reassurance.

She was still awake when she heard her father come in, and, puzzled, she looked at the little clock on the dressing table. A quarter past twelve! An incredible time for him to come in from a mere walk, when he had left the house at seven. To add to the surprise of his coming in so late, she could not but mark the caution with which he mounted the stairs, the wariness with which he walked, heavily on tip-toe, past her door to his own room. Only by straining her ears could she hear his door close. And then she gave herself a mental shake and got up to prepare for bed.

The explanation of her father's late return was quite simple, after all. He had been playing pinochle with some of his cronies, probably in the back of the barbershop, which she knew, was a favorite meeting place for some of the rather raffish citizens who were his particular friends. And with that explanation, she crawled into bed and finally fell asleep.

6

WITH the last of the Saturday baking in the stove, and Annie safely in charge, Megan stripped off her apron, went out of doors, and whistled to the dogs.

They came bounding to her, wild with excitement, knowing that they were to be taken for a walk. They might — and often did — spend hours of each day or night in the woods along the Ridge, but to have her go with them was a treat of which they never tired. The cats came, too, and the chickens fell in behind her and strung out like the tail on a comet, clucking and squawking. The cows came to meet her as she crossed the meadow, and by the time she had reached the fence at the top of the meadow, she was surrounded by what she affectionately and laughingly called her usual three-ring circus.

Reaching the top of the hill, where the big flat stone lay at the foot of the tallest, most majestic pine, she sat down and looked upon the scene about her and found it very fair indeed. It was a peaceful scene in the mild Autumn morning. Here in this sheltered coastal country, winter played a mild hand; there was hardly ever any ice, seldom a killing frost. Two crops a year grew from the farms, and life was peaceful and placid. Or it had been until Alicia Stevenson came to live here. Megan jerked her thoughts away from the unpleasant riddle of Alicia Stevenson, because she had something of far more importance, to herself at least, to think about.

The news of her engagement to Laurence had been accepted without surprise in Pleasant Grove. Everyone had taken it for granted that Megan would sell the farm when she married Laurence. Nobody who knew Jim MacTavish could visualize him running the farm or even living there after Megan was gone. He'd take the money Megan got from the sale and run through it and be 'on' Laurence and Megan's hands for support the rest of his life. Megan was unapologetic for the thought; she was not conscious of any disloyalty towards her father in holding such a thought. She was simply facing facts. She knew him so well that she did not make mistaken plans that maybe Jim would look after himself. She didn't even expect it. She had thought vaguely that perhaps Laurence could invest the proceeds from the sale of the farm in an annuity that would give her father a small income, and protect the principal. But the thought had been merely vague, because not until this moment had she actually faced the prospect of selling the farm.

She looked down at it, the ugly, but beloved old house, set neatly back from the road, with its neat green lawn, the barnyard with its neat red barn and its well-fed, well-tended stock, the two mules and the cows, the pigs, the chickens that provided her with eggs to sell, the cats and the dogs —

Why, she told herself, startled, if she sold the farm she would have to dispose of the cats and the dogs as well as the rest of the stock!

She looked out over the beloved acres of the old farm. Not to be here when the early spring broke, not to go out with tractor and harrow and turn back the rich dark earth, to drop the tiny seeds into the ground and witness that age-old, ever recurring miracle that brought food and sustenance from the dark earth by means of those tiny, hard seeds. She was of the soil; she had been born to it; she had inherited it, not only from her mother but from her mother's people before her; every inch of the place was part of her. Away from it, she would be like something crippled and only half-alive. The strongest, most vital part of her would be left here in these treasured fields and meadows.

Suddenly she felt very tired, but

she had reached her decision. She could not marry Laurence and sell the farm and go to live in a small bungalow with a backyard-garden and one cat and one dog. Her life was here. Somehow, she must make Laurence see that. It wasn't going to be easy, but her mind was made up. And as though the achieving of a decision had relieved her of some great burden, she threw back her shoulders, and stood up, feeling suddenly light and free —

A movement in the backyard behind the Westbrook place caught her startled attention. At first she thought it was merely something white hanging on the clothesline, fluttering in the soft mild wind. And then she realized that it was a human figure, a woman in white, moving oddly, bending as though to pick something up, straightening to fling her arms wide, her head back. At this distance, she could tell nothing more than that. And then suddenly, with a little creeping feeling of discomfort, she realized what the woman was doing — *she was dancing!*

A queer oddly rhythmic dance, grotesque in its lack of grace, clumsy and awkward. The sun glinted on the woman's golden hair, as she bent and postured and straightened and whirled, her arms outflung!

Suddenly a shorter, darker, woman hurried out of the house, put her arm about the dancing figure, and managed to draw it into the house.

Megan shuddered and put her hands over her face for a moment, as though to shut out the remembered figure swaying and posturing and turning. Tom Fallon's poor wife, of course. "Mentally ill," he had said. Her heart twisted with pity for the man who must carry this burden in his heart, a woman beloved, set apart from all the normal things of life, beyond his reach to help. To have to watch her, to know that there was nothing he could do for her — what a horrible thing! She was sick at the thought of what Tom Fallon's life must be, here in this drab, lonely little house, with the picture of his beloved wife as she must have been when they were first married — and now this poor, witless thing!

Her own period of troubled indecision seemed absurd and childish, compared to the horror that must live with Tom Fallon all the days of his life. She went back down the Ridge and across the meadow to the house.

Annie was getting the midday dinner on the table as she came in, and by the time it was ready Jim came down, a little bloodshot and drawn about the mouth, but freshly shaven and neatly dressed.

He was in high good humor as he sat down at the table, but he shuddered when he saw the steaming food.

"A poached egg, Annie, and some toast," he suggested affably.

Annie looked meaningly at the green beans, cooked with tiny squares of salt pork and little potatoes, at the crisp, hot corn muffins, the green salad, the chops done to a delicious brown.

"Yes, sir," she said heavily, and the swinging door to the kitchen shut forcefully behind her.

"Well, my dear," said Jim happily, "I think we're going to he able to get an excellent price for the place. I was talking to Matthews yesterday, and he tells me that we could get twenty thousand."

"We're not going to sell the farm, Dad," Megan told him quietly.

Jim stared at her, unpleasantly surprised.

"My dear girl, what are you talking about?" he demanded sharply. "You haven't already broken your engagement?"

"Not yet. I suppose it will end with that, but I haven't seen Laurence to tell him what I've decided," Megan admitted frankly.

"Well, if it's not asking too much confidence, what *have* you decided?" asked Jim harshly.

"That I can't sell the farm, because I can't imagine living any place else," she told him quite honestly, but if, for a moment, there was a plea for sympathy and understanding in her eyes, it was doomed to failure, for her father was obviously quite angry and in no mood to understand anything but his own disappointment.

Annie put down the poached egg and the crisp, golden brown toast and shot Megan a glance that said she had been listening and that her sympathies were all with Megan.

When the swinging door had closed behind her broad back, Jim said furiously, "Well, you've certainly put me in a tough spot! You might at least have given me some inkling of the way you felt before I gave Matthews the listing on the place."

In swift alarm, Megan said hurriedly, "Oh, Dad, you didn't — "

"I most certainly did," her father told her curtly. "I happened to run into him up at the service station and he was looking for a place for some people who want to move down in here — though God knows why! A more forlorn place to live I can't imagine."

"But if you listed the place and he made you a bona fide offer and you accepted it — " she protested.

"Which is exactly what I did," her father told her with obvious satisfaction in his voice. "And he's going to bring the people down here to settle things the first of the week. I'm afraid we'll have to sell whether you want to or not."

Megan drew a long breath and said quietly, "I don't think so, Dad. The place was left to us jointly; neither can sell without the consent of the other. I am certain that I can't be forced to accept a deal that you and Matthews cooked up without even consulting me."

Her father's face darkened. He had never quite forgiven his wife for leaving her ancestral home jointly to himself and his daughter, instead of to him alone. And he always bitterly resented being reminded of the status of the property.

"Well, perhaps not," he admitted reluctantly. "But of course, we will have to pay him his commission, even though the sale doesn't go through, since it was our fault — yours, rather — and not his, that it did fail! I think it would be much better if we just let the sale go through — don't you? I'm afraid two thousand dollars is rather a lot of money in the present state of our finances — isn't it?"

"Quite a lot," she agreed, pushing back her plate. She had no longer any appetite for the dinner Annie had prepared while she had sat on the Ridge and reached the decision not to sell the old farm. "Maybe Laurence can figure a way out."

"The only way out, if you are stubborn enough not to sell, is to pay Matthews two thousand dollars," her father assured her grimly.

"I haven't exactly found it difficult to spend what little money I've had, either," she answered him as he thrust back his chair, and leaving his breakfast half eaten, went out. She heard the outer door close hard behind him. A minute later Annie came back into the room.

"He's goin' straight to that Stevenson woman," she reported, with relish.

Megan set her teeth hard for a moment and then she drew a deep breath and said quietly, "That will do, Annie."

Annie hesitated, looking at her hard for a moment, and then she said colorlessly, "Yes'm."

She and Annie understood each other without the clumsy medium of words. Megan had ample reason to know what Annie thought of Jim MacTavish; but Annie knew too, that her employer would not permit her to put her dislike and her contempt for him into words. Annie had the worker's contempt for the loafers of the world, star among whom she felt was Jim MacTavish. But too, she respected Megan's refusal to allow her to voice that contempt.

When Annie had gone, Megan sat on for a little at the table, though her appetite for food had long since vanished; and then with sudden decision she got up and went to the telephone, where she called Laurence in Meadersville.

His voice sounded warm and cheerful and eager, as though he was delighted to hear her say, "Larry, this is Megan — I'm in a jam."

His laugh came back to her, thinned by distance.

"Not you, darling," he countered gaily. "I don't believe it — you're covering for somebody else."

"Well, perhaps — in a way," she admitted reluctantly. Then as briefly as she could, she related her father's conversation with Matthews. When she had finished, she asked anxiously, "Do I have to pay Matthews' commission, even if the sale does not go through?"

"Not unless you and your father both signed the papers with him authorizing him to make the sale," Laurence assured her promptly.

"Thank goodness!" said Megan youthfully.

"But, look, Meggie, if Matthews can get you twenty thousand, why don't you want to sell? That's a top price," Laurence pointed out.

"It's just that I don't want to sell at all, Larry," she answered him eagerly.

There was a pause at the other end of the line, and then Laurence asked tautly, "Does that mean you've changed your mind, Meggie — about me?"

"Oh, no, Larry," she answered eagerly, and then added with reluctant honesty, "At least I don't think so — it's something we'll have to talk about — "

"Of course." Laurence was remembering tardily that this was a party line and there were probably two or three interested listeners on the line, and now he became brisk and formal. "Well, anyway, I'll see you tomorrow."

"Come over early and have lunch," Megan invited cordially.

Laurence laughed. "Well, thanks," he accepted, and added matter-of-factly, "I meant to, anyway!"

"Good!" said Megan. "I'll have Annie fry a chicken for you — your way!" she promised.

"Oh, you don't have to lure me with fried chicken," Laurence assured her significantly. When she turned away from the telephone, her spirits were lighter, and she felt as though she had shed the burden of a rather terrifying nightmare. It was good to have someone to turn to in trouble; she had walked alone since her mother's death, for her father had been less than no help at all. Her heart felt very warm towards Laurence as she went about her work that afternoon.

7

THE night was superb. A full moon, silver-white in a pale blue sky, rode high, and beneath the thick dark of the shrubbery on the lawn and the ancient live oaks, the shadows were like soft black plush. Megan's room was flooded with the silver-white light when she awoke, and she lay still for a moment, puzzled to know why she had awakened. And then the sound came again, a knocking at the kitchen door downstairs, a knocking soft, urgent, repeated, insistent.

With her heart hammering with sudden uneasiness, she slid out of bed, thrust her feet into slippers, caught up the cotton robe hanging across the foot of the bed, and went swiftly to the window that overlooked the backyard.

"Who's down there?" she called

quickly, and remembered to wonder why neither Bessie nor Dixie had barked a warning of a stranger's approach.

The man who had been knocking stepped back from the door, and full into the white moonlight, lifting his face to her, and she recognized Tom Fallon.

"I'm terribly sorry to waken you," he said swiftly, and his voice was taut with uneasiness. "But the telephone is out of order — there's been an accident — we want a doctor."

Megan said instantly, "I'll be down in a moment."

There wasn't time to do anything but tie her kimono about her, and to shake back the leaf-brown burnished curls from her face. She went swiftly down the stairs, and unlocked the kitchen door. Tom stepped into the kitchen, clean and tidy and waiting for Annie's breakfast preparations.

"Your wife?" asked Megan.

Tom shook his head and she saw

that his face was white and set. His jaw looked ridged and his eyes were bleak.

"It's Martha, my wife's sister," he said curtly. "She — fell and hurt herself. I have to hurry — they're there alone — both of them completely helpless."

Megan said quickly, "You go back, and I'll call the doctor. If he's not at home, and out on a call somewhere it may take a little time to get him. So let me do it — "

Tom said huskily, "Thanks. You're — you're more than kind."

He turned and went swiftly out into the moon-washed darkness and Megan went to the telephone. The doctor was out, and it took some little time for her to locate him, and then it was with the assurance that it would be an hour at least before he could make the call at the Westbrook place.

Megan put down the telephone and hesitated a moment Then she ran upstairs, got swiftly into outdoor shoes

71

and stockings, a skirt and a light, warm sweater, because the night was chill. She tied a scarf about her head, caught up her little First Aid kit, and let herself out of the house.

She was answering the call of a neighbor's need as instinctively, as thoughtlessly, as had always been Pleasant Grove's custom. People who had been enemies for years, who never spoke when they met, laid aside all personal animosities when the enemy was ill or in trouble, and 'pitched in' to help. It was unthinkable, in Pleasant Grove's creed, that one should do anything else.

She went quickly down the moon-silvered road, crossed the little wooden bridge, and went on up the low hill, turning in at the weed-grown, gateless drive, through shrubbery that had run riot and that tonight gave the house an air of mystery and furtiveness that was almost unpleasant.

She heard the murmur of voices before she knocked, then an instant silence, and the movement of feet coming towards the kitchen door. The door swung open and Tom stood there, his coat discarded, his sleeves rolled up; behind him she saw a kitchen that was spotlessly tidy, though depressingly drab, and a short, stout woman huddled in a chair, her face turned over her shoulder to look at the door.

Megan said to Tom, "Dr. Alden will be here as soon as he can make it. I thought perhaps I might be of some help, before he gets here. I've had First Aid training — "

The woman said harshly, sharply, "Don't let her in, Tom — don't you let her in!"

Tom flushed darkly with embarrassment, and said over his shoulder, "Be quiet, Martha!" And to Megan, holding the door open, he said gratefully, "This is kind of you — but — you needn't — "

"I am always glad to do anything I possibly can for a neighbor," Megan assured him. She crossed the threshold to face the woman, whose dark, angry face and blazing eyes watched her angrily.

"There's nothing you can do, and we can wait perfectly well for Dr. Alden," she stated grimly. "So you'd better go on back home."

Tom turned on her and said through his teeth, "Martha, be quiet — she — she knows."

Martha looked startled, incredulous; and then anger lit up her small, dark eyes even more vividly, and she turned away, her teeth set hard above what must have been a furiously savage anger.

Megan hesitated, looking down at the woman, and Tom bridged the tense, unpleasant moment by saying quietly, "Martha — fell and hurt her ankle. I don't think it is broken, but it is swelling fast and very painful — "

Megan knelt before the woman, and Tom brought a footstool. Without a word to either of them, Martha submitted to their ministrations. Megan was deft and gentle in her movements, and when she had finished, Martha breathed a sigh of relief. Megan saw that her forehead was damp with sweat and that there was a little white line about her mouth. It was obvious that Martha was in great pain, and Megan found it easy to forgive her her rudeness.

"Would you like me to make you a cup of coffee?" suggested Megan gently when she had finished. "Or perhaps a cup of tea?"

Martha wiped her forehead with the back of her hand and said huskily, reluctantly, "Well, I guess you might as well — it would taste good — tea, not coffee."

Megan rose and lit the stove. She was just putting water on to heat when suddenly a cry rang out that was like icy fingers tapping up and down her spine, a cry that chilled the blood and left the heart beating with mad, staggering haste.

"*Tom* — " Martha cried.

Tom nodded and leaped toward a closed door, and opened it. In the fleeting instant before it closed behind him, Megan caught a glimpse of a room daintily and charmingly furnished, and a figure bolt upright in the bed, a figure with gleaming golden hair disheveled about a small white face. And then the door closed, and she could hear Tom murmuring soothing words. Gradually the sobbing that had followed that terrible, wailing cry subsided.

Megan drew a deep breath and turned to see Martha watching her with a savage intensity that made her think of a crouching beast protecting its young. It was a crazy thought and she tried to dismiss it the moment it struck her, but Martha only watched her the more closely, her mouth set like a steel trap.

Megan said quietly, her voice not quite steady, "Mrs. Fallon must have had a bad dream. They can frighten one to pieces."

Martha's eyes widened a little, and

her expression relaxed ever so slightly. She was plainly startled, and a little suspicious, but as Megan scalded out the teapot, Martha nodded slowly and said uneasily, "Yes — it must have been that. She's — she's — ill and doesn't sleep much, and my fall excited her and — yes, she must have had a nightmare."

She watched Megan with sharp secretive eyes, avid for any change of expression that might tell her that Megan did not believe her.

Megan poured the boiling water into the teapot, and said, her tone deliberately quiet and natural, "Perhaps Mrs Fallon would like a cup of hot milk? Would it soothe her, do you think?"

Martha hesitated. "It might, at that," she agreed. "Tom could get her to drink it."

Megan nodded and poured milk into a saucepan. When it was hot, she filled a glass and went to the door with it. She knocked with the tips of her fingers, very lightly, and a moment later, Tom opened the door. She all but cried out at the sight of his face, white and ravaged and stiff with despair. But she made herself speak casually and offer him the glass of milk. He took it from her with a flash of gratitude that was touching.

She came back to the stove, and tested the tea. Martha said it was "just right" and Megan poured her a cup of it. They were drinking the last of the tea when there was the sound of a car in the drive, and a moment later, Dr. Alden, stout, elderly, tired-looking, the typical country doctor, came briskly in.

"Hello — you here?" he greeted Megan cheerfully, looking at Martha curiously. "What seems to be the trouble?"

"There's no seeming about it," Martha told him tartly. "I fell and twisted my ankle somehow, and Tom would have it that he must call a doctor."

He straightened at last, saying briskly, "Painful, but not dangerous. Just keep up the treatment, Megan, and see she stays off her feet for the next three or four days — or a week. I don't look for any complications."

As he turned towards the door, Tom came out of that room that was in such sharp contrast to the drab, cheerless house, and shook hands with the doctor, thanking him for his trip.

"You didn't really need me, though," Dr. Alden assured him, with a gesture towards Megan. "She'd done all that was necessary before I came. She can continue the treatment, and the patient will be up and around in a few days — if she stays off that foot until then."

Tom walked with him out to the car. When he came back, he said to Megan, "I don't know how to thank you — "

"There's nothing to thank me for — "

"I know — it's just the neighborly spirit of Pleasant Grove," he told her, smiling.

Megan was tucking things into her kit, her eyes and hands intent.

Tom said, "I'll see you home, Megan, of course."

"No," said Megan firmly. "You are needed here. It's not far and the dogs are waiting for me outside. You stay here. Goodnight, Miss — Martha, and I hope you'll be much better in the morning."

Martha did not answer. Tom walked with Megan out of the warm, lamplit kitchen and to the drive. He walked beside her to the road, and there she turned and said, "This is far enough. You mustn't leave them alone."

Bessie and Dixie were leaping about her in delight of this strange nighttime walk, and Tom yielded to her insistence that she did not need him.

"I don't know how to thank you, or how to apologize for Martha," he said awkwardly, in such obvious misery that Megan felt her heart twist in sympathy. "She — she doesn't really mean it. She's just — well, fought so hard for her sister's — secret that she's not herself."

"Please don't say any more." Megan begged him quickly. "I understand perfectly. Get her to bed and see that she takes one of those tablets Dr. Alden left. It will help her to sleep."

"I will," Tom promised, holding out his hand. He stood still for a moment, looking deep into her eyes, as they lifted to his in the moonlight. And suddenly as they stood there in a world made up of the black and silver mosaic of moonlight and shadows, Megan felt a queer shock touch her heart, almost as though inadvertently she had touched a live electric wire. The next moment the queer feeling was gone and she had said good night to him and was walking down the road.

From the moment when she had awakened in the moonlight to hear that queer little tapping noise at the door downstairs, until she had stood in the kitchen at the Westbrook place, and caught that startling glimpse of a room dainty and luxurious, that white-clad golden-haired figure sitting bolt upright in bed, small white face convulsed with terror, she had hardly had a moment to think.

But now, sorting out the various emotions she had experienced, she shivered at the glimpse of what Tom Fallon's life must be in that drab little house with the two women, one of them lovely and mad, and the older woman whose love and devotion to the golden-haired creature had warped her own disposition until she herself was far from normal.

Suddenly she remembered something he had said when he had first come to the house to call the doctor. At the moment she had not realized the implication of the words. He had said, "I have to get back — they're both completely helpless." Well, Martha was, of course, because of her ankle. But his wife? Once more she saw that weirdly moving, grotesquely posturing white-clad figure on the back lawn of the old place saw it move with stiff, awkward steps, weaving and dipping — and then the short, stocky, dark clad figure coming out to draw the white-clad one back into the house.

And then she told herself curtly, "Stop being a fool! He only meant his wife was helpless because of her — mental condition. He didn't mean that she was physically helpless — not bedridden or anything like that."

She let herself quietly into the house, grateful for its warmth and darkness. But as she moved across the kitchen towards the hall, there was a sudden sound and the light flashed up and she faced her father.

She gave a startled gasp, and tried to laugh. "Oh did I wake you?" she said. "I'm sorry — I tried to be very cautious — "

"Sly would be the word I'd use," said her father with insolence and sharp accusation in his voice, his eyes taking her in from the top of her hair, tumbled where she had just removed the closely wrapped scarf, to the tips of her shoes dusty from the quarter-mile walk along the unpaved road. "I wouldn't have believed it if I hadn't seen it with my own eyes! How long has this — this disgraceful business been going on?" he added, his voice thick with righteous anger.

Megan stared at him, wide-eyed and bewildered by the depth of his anger.

"I don't know what you're talking about — " she began.

"Don't try to lie out of it," he snapped at her furiously. "I heard that — that — Fallon man come to the back door and tap, for all the world like some — street bum beneath the window of his — light o' love! And I heard you go down to him — I couldn't believe that you would really leave the house with him — "

"If you heard so much, Dad, without even sufficient interest in my affairs to ask a simple question, then you must have heard me telephone Dr. Alden — "

84

"I don't propose to have my intelligence insulted by some weak-kneed silly lie!" he blazed at her.

"You're going to listen to me just the same," her voice cut across his. "Mr. Fallon came here to use the telephone to call a doctor. His sister-in-law, who lives with them and takes care of his invalid wife, had fallen and hurt her ankle. I went over, as any good neighbor would, and made use of some of my First Aid training — "

Her father sneered at her.

"And that was exactly what I meant by some weak-kneed, silly lie," he told her shortly. "You sneaked out of this house and were gone with that man — a married man, whose wife is a bedridden invalid, and were gone three hours — "

He was lashing himself into a fury, and Megan eyed him for a moment, with a look beneath which his self-righteous bluster faded a little.

"You'd like to make it impossible for me to stay on in Pleasant Grove, Dad?"

she suggested quietly. "You'd go even to that length to try to force me to sell — "

"You are being insolent and brazen," her father cut in loftily. "I admit frankly that if you're in love with this married man, the wisest thing for you to do is put as much distance between you and him as possible."

Megan's eyes were wide and incredulous.

"In love with Tom Fallon?" she repeated as though she could not believe the absurd charge.

"But — I'm willing to be broadminded about tonight, Meggie," her father said at last. "You've always been a good daughter, and if you tell me there was nothing wrong in your going out with Fallon — I'll take your word for it."

"That's good of you!" Megan forced the words through her teeth, her voice trembling.

Her father shot her a swift, vindictive look.

"But of course, only on condition

that you see no more of the man, and that you sell out and we both get as far from this place as possible," he went on sternly. "You've got a chance to marry a fine young fellow, and live a much easier life than you've known here. Farming is no job for a girl — "

Once more, she dared risk only a few words, lest the threatening tears overwhelm her.

"I'm not selling the farm, Dad — that's final," she told him and managed to get up the stairs and to her own room before she gave way to tears.

She admitted now, forlornly, in the first moment of her emotional reaction, that she had never liked her father. But now she hated him! The thought shocked her. But she had to admit its truth.

All through the years when she had been growing up, and as each year had given her more awareness of conditions between her father and mother, she had been growing to this point where she must hate him. He had hurt her mother over and over again; she could remember coming home from school, gay and blithe with the small day's happenings, the happiness of a child, to find her mother red-eyed and white-faced, offering to the child a hard-won composure that did not deceive the growing Megan in the least. She always knew, at such times, with a sick sense of helplessness, that her father had done something to make her mother unhappy. There were many such occasions; yet it was so easy for him to make her mother light up with a glow of happiness. Because, she knew her mother had loved him to the day of her death.

He had always hated the farm; he had tried again and again to get her mother to sell. He had wanted to go into business in a city somewhere. Megan had heard his magnificent plans for 'investing' the money the farm would bring; at that time, while Megan had been growing up the farm would have brought very little, and steadfastly her mother had refused to sell.

"Land is a security, Meggie," her mother had told her, long before Megan had been old enough to understand. "While you've got a roof over your head and a bit of land to take care of you, you're always safe. Never forget that, Meggie."

And Megan had not. With every year since her mother's death, she had fought off her father's efforts to sell; but she was tired of fighting, and the tears came, as she seldom allowed them to.

8

LATE Sunday morning Megan walked up to the bus stop to meet Laurence, and when he came swinging towards her, his face lit up with eager delight at the sight of her. The day was mild and warm, the sunlight golden on her russet-brown head, but all Laurence said as he greeted her was an eager, "Hello!"

"Hello," she answered, and laughed a little because it was such a glorious morning and she liked being with Laurence.

They walked hand in hand back down the road to the house, and then Laurence said, "I've been shut up in what passes for a city, in these parts, for quite a bit — couldn't we walk down through the meadow and over to the Ridge before lunch?"

"We'll probably just about have

time," Megan answered him lightly. They crossed the backyard, and went down through the meadow with, of course, the inevitable accompaniment of dogs and cats and chickens and cows.

They went hand in hand up the path and to the flat rock that crowned the very top of the hill. Megan sat down and Laurence followed her to the rock. They sat close together for a moment, looking out over the scene spread below them.

Megan knew the thought that was in his mind, and she tried hard to marshal all her arguments so that he could understand; but when he turned his head and looked at her, and smiled, he said quietly, "I can't say I blame you for not being willing to give all this up! We are going to be very happy here."

Megan felt as though she had taken a step in the dark and plunged headlong into space. She could only stare at him, wide-eyed, her mouth open a little.

Laurence laughed and leaned forward and kissed her.

"Because, make no mistake about it, my love — you're going to marry me, whether we live in Meadersville or Pleasant Grove!"

There were quick tears in her eyes, but she smiled tremulously.

"Thank you for understanding, Larry," she told him huskily. "It's — a tremendous relief."

Laurence frowned as though not quite sure that he liked that.

"You mean you didn't think I *would* understand?" he protested. "Well, for Pete's sake, why not? After all, we've grown up together. Don't you suppose I've come to understand what the place means to you? And to be frank with you — I'm kind of fond of the old place myself! Never having owned a square foot of real estate in my life, the thought of becoming a landowner — in partnership, anyway — seems pretty swell!"

He grinned at her and said hastily,

"Not, of course that I want you to get the idea that I'm merely marrying you for your farm. I'd marry you if you didn't have a foot of land!"

She laughed and let him kiss her. And at first, that seemed quite satisfactory to Laurence; but after a little he let her go, and sat looking down at the rich dark earth, where his heel was absently digging a hole.

"Then you're not in love with me, after all," he said quietly, and there was a note in his voice that caught at her heart.

She stared at him, blinking in amazement.

"What in the world — why do you — " she stammered.

"I'm not exactly a blind fool, Meggie," he said evenly. "I admit I don't know a lot about women; but I do know when a girl is in love, she is not only kissed — but kisses, in return."

The color burned in Megan's face, but her eyes met his straightly.

"I — kissed you, Larry," she told him unsteadily.

He shook his head.

"You let me kiss you, Meggie," he returned. "There's a big difference."

There was a silence and then she said unevenly, "I'm — sorry, dear."

He shook his head.

"There's nothing for you to be sorry about, Meggie If you don't love me, you don't, and it's plain that you don't." His voice sounded tired.

Megan sat very still for a moment, her hands clenched tightly in her lap.

"I'm — very fond of you, Larry," she said then.

Laurence smiled at her, a smile that had in it nothing that was mirthful and a great deal that was sad.

"Thanks, Meggie," he answered quietly. "But — I'm afraid that's not quite enough."

And then, taking her breath away by the unexpectedness of it, he asked, "Is there someone else, Meggie?"

Wide-eyed, she met his glance.

"But — how could there be someone else?" she protested.

His smile was as mirthless as ever.

"*I'm* asking *you*," he reminded her.

Suddenly she was flushed and confused and her face was burning; it was incredible, but she could no longer meet his eyes.

"It's — it's a crazy question, Larry — I *don't* know anyone else," she pointed out.

"That's not quite flattering," he assured her, and now he seemed amused at her confusion and her bewilderment. "Never mind, darling. We'll let it go, for now. But I wouldn't want you to marry me, Meggie, unless you felt a little about me as I feel about you. I guess I don't quite expect you to be — well, as much in love with me as I am with you; the wise people who claim to know about such things claim that one person in every marriage cares more deeply than the other. I don't mind a bit if I love you more than you love me. Maybe that's the way it should be. I'm afraid I'm not wise enough to decide that. I only know that unless you're — more than just fond of me — it wouldn't work out."

Megan said faintly, "You mean you want to break off the engagement, Larry?"

Laurence studied her for a moment.

"Do *you*, Meggie?" he asked quietly.

"Why — why — no, Larry — of course not," she stammered, and put out a hand in a helpless gesture. "I — I think I've always expected that we'd be married some day. It's — well, I've sort of grown up with that thought. Maybe — could it be that that's the reason you don't think I love you enough?"

"It isn't that I *think* you don't love me, Meggie — I *know* you don't," he told her. "I've tried to kid myself that you did, and tried to hope that once we were actually engaged, you'd — well warm up to me a little. But when you thought of setting a date for our marriage and realized that you couldn't give up the farm or the dogs and cats and cows and chickens, to make a new life with me somewhere — or anywhere! — that was all I needed to convince me that you're not ready to marry me yet. If you loved me as I love you, Meggie, nothing in the world would be as important to you as being with me — anywhere, anyhow."

He broke off as though searching for words with which to make his thoughts clear to her.

"It isn't that I'd want you to make even the smallest sacrifice to be with me, Meggie," he pointed out. "It's just that if you loved me the only way I could want you to — you'd be willing to sacrifice anything and everything just so that we could be together. Do you understand, Meggie?"

She was still for a moment, and then reluctantly she nodded and said faintly, "Yes, darling — I understand."

"Then we'll leave it at that, for the present," said Laurence as he stood up and drew her to her feet. "And now Annie will be sending out a searching party for us if we don't hurry," he added, smiling, deliberately breaking the growing tension, struggling for a lighter tone.

Suddenly, a mist of tears in her eyes, Megan turned to him impulsively, put her hands on either side of his lean, pleasant brown face and stood on tiptoe to set her mouth, cool and fresh and sweet, on his. Involuntarily his arms went about her, holding her close and hard against him. His mouth on hers was urgent, demanding, seeking a response that after a moment, he knew with a sick certainty was not there. And then he released her, smiled at her, his face pale and set, and half under his breath he said huskily, "Thanks, darling."

They went back down across the meadow, hand in hand, the dogs leaping gaily about them, the cats stepping daintily, pausing now and then to rub against their ankles and purr loudly their satisfaction in the way things were.

Annie was just finishing the last preparations for the mid day dinner when they reached the house, and Jim came in, well-groomed and debonair, quite as usual, as they were ready to sit down.

He greeted Laurence with an urbanity that was almost patronizing, but after a few moments he said briskly, "Well, Larry, my boy, I hope you've been able to persuade this girl of mine to be sensible."

"Megan seems to feel that it would be best for us not to be married for another year," Laurence said gently. "And therefore, she will want to run the place herself this year, at least."

Jim looked sharply at him and then at Megan, his thick brows drawn together in a dark, angry scowl.

"Another year, eh?" he said at last. "Sorry — I thought you two were in love with each other and had been waiting several years for you to get a start so that you could be married!"

"As I said before, we are sensible

young people, Meggie and I. Slow and sure is our motto," Laurence told him.

Jim's jaw set and he made a pretense of eating, but after a little he looked at his watch, thrust his chair back, and asked to be excused. They heard the outer door close behind him with a bang that threatened its old-fashioned glass panel.

"I'm afraid he's upset." Laurence's words were wry with understatement. "He won't try to make things difficult for you?"

Megan's eyes widened in surprise.

"Goodness, no — and if he does, it won't matter. I'm not in the least afraid of him!" She laughed at the very idea.

Laurence nodded. "But if there should ever be anything to — well, to make you feel you need help — you'll remember my telephone number?" he reminded her.

"Thanks, Larry — you're sweet!" Megan's voice was warm with affection and gratitude.

Laurence grinned wryly. "Sure — Old Dog Tray — that's me!" he assured her.

Both were deeply grateful for Annie's arrival, bearing plates of cherry pie heaped with thick whipped cream, and fresh coffee. In Laurence's enthusiastic appreciation of the picture the generous slices of pie made, and in Annie's beaming delight of his flattery, the moment died.

9

IN the next few weeks, life in Pleasant Grove, on the surface at least, was entirely normal. But there were currents underneath that popped above the surface now and then, and to no one's very keen surprise, Alicia Stevenson seemed to have a large part in them. Her malicious tongue, her sly little smile that hinted at so much she did not say, the way she had of always being in the very middle of any untoward event, filled people with angry unease.

"It's got so a body ain't safe in their own home nights, with that woman snoopin' around," Annie complained to Megan one afternoon as they sat sewing before the fire that the chill rain made very welcome. She shot Megan an oblique look and then came out frankly with what was in her mind.

"I can't imagine what your paw sees in her, anyhow."

Megan dropped the tablecloth she was mending and stared at Annie.

"My father?" she gasped incredulously.

"The way your paw's runnin' after that Stevenson woman is the talk of the town."

"That will do, Annie," said Megan sharply, and the subject was dropped.

That night, when Megan and her father were alone in the house, Megan said quietly, "I understand, Dad, that you've been seeing a lot of Mrs. Stevenson?"

Jim looked up at her from his newspaper, and his eyes darkened with anger. "Have you any objections?" he demanded curtly.

"None at all," she answered him evenly. "It's just that I was a little surprised, that's all — to hear a thing like that from the neighbors, instead of from you — "

"If you're prying, trying to find out about my intentions towards Mrs.

Stevenson," Jim said distinctly, a little malicious light in his eyes, "I have no objection to telling you the truth. I hope to marry Mrs. Stevenson — as soon as I can persuade her! She's selling her place, and I think we can make her happy here, don't you?"

He looked about the shabby old living room, humming a little tune under his breath, blandly aware of the emotion his words aroused in her, amused and also pleased that he had startled her so unpleasantly.

"You would bring *her* — here?" Megan gasped, appalled.

Jim's eyebrows went up in pretended surprise, though his eyes laughed at her.

"And where else would a man take his wife, if not to his own home?" he asked. "You aren't forgetting that it *is* my home — quite as much as it is yours?"

Megan sat very still, stunned with the unexpectedness of the blow.

"Of course," Jim went on after a

moment, "when Matthews was so sure he could get twenty thousand for this place, Alicia and I planned to keep her place and live there, because her place won't bring over seven or eight thousand. But when you decided not to sell — well, Alicia gave the listing of hers to Matthews, and we feel that we can all be quite cozy here together."

Megan drew a hard breath. "You know that wouldn't work out, Dad," she said.

"I think you're taking a very unreasonable attitude, my dear," said her father gently, malice twinkling in his eyes. "After all, having Alicia here will make things much easier for you. She will take over the management of the house, while you can give all your time to your beloved farming! I think it will be a very good arrangement, all around."

Megan studied him sharply. "So Annie is to be fired and Alicia is to take over the house — but I may stay on if I'm willing to confine myself to the outside work — is that it?"

"Well, it seems to be a very good arrangement," her father assured her, innocently, yet with malice in his eyes. She had seen him like this with her mother, gentle, mild, yet with that same look in his eyes, goading her beyond endurance —

"It won't work, Father," she told him flatly.

"No?" His tone and smile were tantalizing.

"No! I'm not selling! And that's that!" she told him again, her jaw hard and set, her voice unshaken.

Her father looked at her and then with a shrug, went back to his paper, his expression unreadable.

Megan got up when she saw that it was obvious he had had his way. She went upstairs to her own room, and sat down on the edge of the bed. Her hands were cold and shaking, and there was a bitter, brackish taste in her mouth.

Her father had beaten her, of course.

Because if he brought Alicia here, she, Megan, could not stay. They would see to that between them. No roof, no matter how ample, could ever be big enough to shelter both Alicia Stevenson and herself. So whether she sold the farm or not — she would have to leave it. There was no other way out.

She got up suddenly and caught up her sweater. The night was mild for winter, yet there was a dampness and a chill in it that made the sweater, and the scarf about her head, very welcome, as she stepped from the back door into the yard.

The moon was up, but it was thin and cold looking, though together with the starlight, it made it possible for her to follow the path she felt she could have taken blindfolded on the darkest night.

The meadow was washed with the thin cold moonlight, but under the trees the darkness was so intense that she had to feel her way from moonlit patch to moonlit patch — until she reached the flat stone beneath the tallest pine; and as she reached it, her heart turned over in her breast, and terror clutched at her, for there was a sudden movement and a shadow moved in the darkness, and she knew that she was not alone. The next moment the shadow had moved swiftly into a patch of moonlight, and she saw it white on Tom Fallon's face.

"I frightened you — I'm sorry — " he apologized.

Megan managed an unsteady laugh. "And I imagine I frightened you, too," she answered him.

"Well, as a matter of fact, you did," he admitted. Then as the moonlight touched her white face he added hurriedly, concerned: "Why, what's happened? You're ill — "

"Oh, no — just — well, upset — and ever since I was a child I've brought my troubles, big and little, to this spot and tried to find a way out of them! It's a habit that's hard to break," she added with an attempted gaiety that had an almost macabre quality.

"Of course." He was pleasantly matter-of-fact and the very calmness of his voice lay like a soothing hand on her jumbled emotions. "By the way, would this be a suitable time to offer my congratulations and best wishes? I hear you're being married very soon."

And to Megan's own horror, and Tom's shocked surprise, she burst into tears!

After a stunned moment, Tom put his arm about her and held her close, as though she were a frightened, bewildered child, and his soothing words were the words one would have used to a grieving child.

He let her cry for a little, and when she sat up and became conscious of his arm about her, and scarlet with embarrassment, he said, with a wry smile, "Funny — I can't imagine a girl like you being bowled over by a lover's quarrel. Because if he's the sort of man a girl like you could love, then he's got too much sense to let you get away from him. He'll come grovelling back tomorrow, begging you to forgive him for no matter what it was you quarrelled about."

"I only wish it was something that could be settled as easily as that," she confessed miserably.

Tom looked at her sharply, frowning a little.

"My father is going to marry Alicia Stevenson," she told him levelly, and so strong was the bond of friendship between them that it did not occur to her to be surprised that she should confide in him.

She heard him swear under his breath, but after a moment, he tried to offer comfort. "Well, of course I suppose she's a very attractive woman — and your father is lonely — "

"And she is selling her place and coming to live with us," she went on.

"Oh, good Lord, you can't live with her — "

"Either that, or I have to agree to sell the farm, and she and father will live in her house."

"And you don't want to sell the farm, or go away from it." Tom understood that without any words from her. "I've gathered since I've known you how much the place means to you — "

He broke off, hesitated, and then asked reluctantly, "But if you're going to be married very soon, wouldn't you be leaving the place anyway?"

"I'm — not going to be married — very soon — not for another year, at least, and even then, we planned to live on the farm."

Tom nodded and sat silent.

She found it very soothing to sit there with him, in silence. It was surprising to discover that they knew each other well enough for silence to be pleasant and companionable so that speech was unnecessary.

They talked quietly, after that interval of peace and stillness. She asked about Martha and he told her that Martha had completely recovered. She asked, hesitantly, about Mrs. Fallon, and he told her, his mouth taut and tired, that there was no change there.

"She's — completely helpless, of course, and there is no change mentally," he added wearily.

"You mean — she can't leave her bed? Can't get around by herself?" asked Megan, remembering with a feeling of chill, the morning when she had sat here and had watched that grotesquely posturing figure on the back lawn.

"She hasn't been out of bed in months and months," he told her heavily. "The doctors say that there is a thin chance of her recovery. That's why we can't bear to — send her away. If I had the money to pay for a private sanitarium — " He shrugged and his hands clenched into hard, tight fists. "But I can't turn her over to a state institution. Not while there's the smallest, faintest, tiniest hope that she can ever be made well again."

Megan asked uneasily, "But shouldn't she be having treatments?"

"She's had treatments for the past four years," Tom answered wearily. "Everything possible has been done, and a few months ago the doctors told me that the only hope was to get her away somewhere quiet, among new scenes, and just to try to build up her physical condition. That might help to restore the lost mental health, but they couldn't guarantee it. She — went to pieces when our son was born — dead."

Megan said, her voice shaken and ragged with pity, "I'm so terribly sorry — "

Unconsciously she had put out her hand to touch him, and as his hand closed over it and held it hard for a moment, she heard him mutter something — she couldn't be sure what.

They were still for a little, and Megan wondered uneasily about his saying that his wife had not been out of bed in months. She knew that she had seen her, a slim white form, the sunlight gleaming gold on her head, dancing a weird, grotesque dance — a dance interrupted by Martha who had taken the white figure into the house.

Did Tom know, she wondered? Did he try to conceal the fact that his wife was not a helplessly bedridden invalid, in the hope of convincing people that, while she was a 'mental case,' she was completely harmless? Of course he and Martha were doing everything humanly possible to keep anybody in Pleasant Grove from knowing that his wife *was* a 'mental case' —

She stood up suddenly and said, "I have to go — I shouldn't have come, at all, but habit it strong."

"I'm glad you did," Tom told her quietly. "And I hope you didn't mind finding me here."

"Of course not. There's room on the Ridge for both of us — and who knows? Maybe we'll both find solutions to our problems here," she answered as she turned to go. "No, you mustn't come with me — "

"Only to the fence," Tom told her. "From there on, you have moonlight clear to your back door and I can watch until you go into the house and know that you're safe."

There was a look in his face that made the protest stop on her lips. She nodded and they walked together to the fence. When she had crossed the meadow and stood at the little foot-log that bridged the small, busy creek, she turned to look back and saw him still standing there. She threw up her arm in a little gesture that said good night and caught the flicker of his return gesture. And then with her heart considerably lighter than it had been when she left the house, she went back in and up the stairs to her own room.

The house was dark and silent. There was no thread of light beneath her father's door, and she was surprised, when she reached her own room, to discover that she'd been gone two hours.

She felt a little ashamed now of the

violence of emotion that had sent her flying from the house to the Ridge; in the face of the grief and heartache that Tom carried with him twenty-four hours of the day, seven days a week, her own seemed trivial.

She heard the downstairs door open and her father start up the stairs. There was something in the stealth, the furtiveness of his tread on the stairs, and the way he opened his door, inching it shut, that roused her more than noise would have done.

She listened at her father's door, and when she heard only a soft, rustling sound, she tapped and asked, "Is that you Father?"

"Who the blazes did you think it was?" he snapped at her.

"I was afraid it might be a burglar — "

"Oh, for love of — what the devil would a burglar want here? I fell asleep over my paper downstairs, and tried to get upstairs without waking you. Hereafter, I'll see to it that you are awakened." There was something odd about his voice that she couldn't quite distinguish. He seemed to be breathing hard, as though he had been running or were laboring under; some terrific excitement.

"Go on to bed!" he called to her sharply, and she turned and went back to her room.

But as she got into bed, the puzzle went with her. He had said he had fallen asleep over his paper; but that would have meant he had fallen asleep with the light burning, and there had been no light burning in the house when she had come in. Also, she had heard the downstairs front door open when he came in. He had not been asleep in the living room — he had been outdoors somewhere.

10

IT was near noon the following day and Megan was busy in her garden when a sudden sharp scream of terror rent the peaceful, mild air.

Megan jerked to her feet as the scream came again — from the direction of Alicia's house, and now she saw a girl whom she recognized as Betty Hendrix, whose father owned a dairy, come stumbling down the path from Alicia's house.

Men and women ran towards her down the road, but it was Megan who reached her first and caught the trembling, white-faced girl and held her, as Betty screamed again, and, with the comfort of Megan's arms about her, burrowed her head into Megan's shoulder and burst into shuddering, sobbing laughter.

"What in the world — " somebody

asked. One of the men ran up the walk to the house, stepping over the milk pail whose contents had splashed over the porch, and looked through the half-open door of Alicia's house.

He gave a yell and stepped back. Then others crowded close and looked in and stepped instantly back as though they had received a blow.

The first man who had reached the place — Bill Logan, it was — pulled the door shut and said sternly, "Mustn't anybody go in there till the police get here. Might mess up a clue or something. Somebody go call the law."

"But what *is* it? What's happened?" cried Megan.

"Miz' Stevenson's been — murdered," said Bill, swallowing hard and looking a little green.

There was a stunned moment of silence and then a little buzz ran around the crowd, and the word 'murder' was the only word that could be distinguished in that buzz.

It was a day never to be forgotten in Pleasant Grove. There was the arrival of old Squire Etheridge, who represented 'the law' in Pleasant Grove, embodying in his ample, elderly frame the justice of the peace and constable. His duty heretofore had been no greater than to sentence chicken thieves and draw up peace warrants between rival factions of a family feud. Later, there was the arrival, at a breakneck speed, of the familiar dusty blue and white sedan that was the symbol of the county police. Throughout the day the crowd increased. By the time the children began to come home from school, and added their own bright, eager faces and piping voices to the shifting crowd, the ambulance had taken away the body of Alicia Stevenson, the doors and windows of the cottage had been locked, and a county officer was on guard.

Tom, stopping on his way from school to pick up his daily supply of milk and eggs, paused for a moment to say, distressed and unhappy, "It's a terrible thing. I can't help feeling terribly sorry for her — alone there. She must have been terrified."

Megan said, in a small, strangled voice, one hand at her throat, "Oh — don't!"

"I'm sorry," Tom said compassionately. "It must have been very unpleasant for you all day with that mob — "

"I hated her — and now she's dead — and I'm so ashamed," Megan confessed humbly.

"They say it happened before midnight," Megan told him thickly. "Perhaps she — she might have screamed — perhaps if I'd been at home — " Her voice broke and she was silent, her teeth sunk hard in her lower lip, her eyes sick and frightened, dark with horror.

Tom came into the kitchen and put his hand on her arm and gave her a little shake. "Stop that!" he ordered sternly. "Even if you had been at home — even if you'd been down here in the living room, you could not have heard her. And in your room upstairs at the back of the house — can't you see how foolish you're being, darling?"

The little endearment slipped out. Yet the moment, the second, after it had been spoken it seemed to crash in both their ears with the sound of doom. His face went white and set and his eyes were bitter and tragic.

Megan caught her breath and looked up at him, her eyes wide and dazed, incredulous. There was a pause between them that could have been a matter of seconds; yet to each of them it seemed to stretch endlessly.

And then Tom said, his voice harsh and very low, "Yes, I said 'darling' — I've thought it often enough."

"Oh — *no!*" Megan said in a small, choked whisper.

Tom straightened. His face looked as though it had been carved out of granite.

"Of course not — it never happened! I didn't say it — I never even think it.

Forget it, will you?" said Tom in that harsh, strained voice. He took up the milk and the basket of eggs and went swiftly out of the house. The sound of his footsteps on the old broken-brick walk were the most final sounds Megan had ever heard in all her life. She stood listening until the last one had died to silence, and then she leaned, weak and shaking against the cabinet behind her and put her cold, trembling hands over her face.

She became conscious of Annie's presence, when Annie said very quietly, her old voice gentle and warm with tenderness, "Your paw's home, honey."

She was too dazed to wonder how long Annie had been there, to wonder how much of that taut little scene Annie had witnessed. Somehow that didn't matter at the moment. She only knew that she must accept Annie's words as a warning and pull herself together before she faced her father.

He came into the dining room, moving wearily, and when he had seated himself, he looked straight at her across the table and said sternly, "Yes, I know about it. We won't discuss it, if you don't mind."

"Of course not," she answered, accepting the dish Annie offered her, and serving herself without in the least knowing what the food was. She managed to eat, without the faintest awareness of what she was eating.

Her father was equally silent. He was pale and there were haggard circles beneath his eyes and his hands were not quite steady. And she did not know when the evil, staggering thought began to creep slyly into her mind; when she began to remember the unusual stealth and caution with which he had let himself into the house last night; the way he had climbed the stairs on tiptoe; the way his door had closed behind him. Suddenly the thought stood clear and hot in her mind: *where had he been?*

It had been after one o'clock when she had come in. That mysterious grapevine by which a secret whispered in the kitchen of a house at one end of town, will reach the farthermost house on the other side of town, in any small place like Pleasant Grove, reported that the doctor felt Mrs. Stevenson had been killed some time between ten o'clock and midnight! And she, Megan MacTavish, had been on the Ridge with another woman's husband from eleven o'clock until almost one!

Her father had come into the house a bit later.

The silent meal ended and she helped Annie clear the table. When Annie refused her help with the dishes, she went reluctantly into the living room and sat down in the chair opposite her father, in front of the small, cheerful fire, and took up her basket of mending. But she could not hold her hands steady, though she managed to thread a needle. And then she saw that her father was watching her covertly, out of the corners of his eyes, and that when she looked straight at him, his eyes dropped almost guiltily to the paper.

She put down the sewing basket. Her mouth was dry, her throat felt constricted with horror, and a creeping fear bred of that slow, evil thought was spreading through her mind. Suddenly, almost as though someone else spoke the words, she asked in a fearful whisper, "Father — did *you* do it?"

She caught her breath and could not believe she had spoken, though the words seemed to quiver in letters of fire between them. Her father stiffened with a little jerk. His face was white and hard and his eyes were veiled, so that she could not guess his thoughts.

For a moment that seemed a century long his eyes met hers, and then he said very softly, "No, my dear — did *you*?"

"Father!" It was a shocked, incredulous gasp that came scarcely above her breath. "How — how can you even — *think* — "

Her father lifted his shoulders in a

gesture that was not quite a shrug and he drawled coolly, "Why not? You seemed perfectly willing to believe I had!"

"Oh no, Dad." In that breathless moment the endearing diminutive came easily from her tongue. "I didn't think you had — I couldn't ever believe you had — "

"Yet you put the question very easily," he reminded her dryly.

"It — it was only that I heard you come in last night — a little after one — "

"A few minutes after you came in, if I remember," said her father calmly, his eyes never leaving her white, ravaged face.

There was a stillness between them, a throbbing moment of silence that screamed unspeakable things, that hinted unimaginable horrors.

Jim went on smoothly, "Of course, there's no likelihood that we should be in any way connected with this terrible affair. Neither of us had any motive to want Alicia out of the way — that is, *I* had none. I hoped to marry her!"

She stared at him, caught by some odd note in his voice. And after a moment he answered the look in her eyes, "Of course if it should become known that you were violently opposed to my marrying her, that you resented the thought of having her here in the house, and had been unable to persuade me to give up my plans to marry her — well — " Once again he lifted his shoulders in that gesture that was not quite a shrug, but that was an effective dismissal.

Megan drew a long hard breath.

"You know I couldn't possibly have — " She set her breath against the sob that clutched at her throat.

"Of course, my dear — I know that you are completely incapable of any such deed of violence!" her father assured her, and there was a warmth that was very close to tenderness in his voice. "But it won't be what *I* know that will count, Megan — it will be what we can prove — or disprove!"

She hesitated and he said quietly, "Megan, if it becomes known that you and I were not in bed and asleep — that you were out on the Ridge with Fallon — it's not only going to be extremely unpleasant for you, but it's going to finish him, once and for all. He'll never be able to get another job as a teacher no matter how innocent and accidental your meeting was. People will remember Alicia's little thrust about your spending 'hours together on the Ridge,' and people are good at adding two and two and getting six or seven."

Megan said quietly, "Where were you, Father?"

He sat very still for a moment, his eyes clinging to hers, and she thought he scarcely seemed to breathe. And then he said casually, "I went for a walk."

As proof that he had had his say on the subject and no intention of speaking again, he got up and left the room. She heard him go up the stairs and along the hall, and then his door closing behind him. But she sat on alone before the dying fire, shivering as though a cold wind had blown over her.

She couldn't believe that her father had killed Alicia Stevenson. It was an incredible thought; but he *had* been out of the house, and he was very anxious that no one should know about that. And she thought of herself and Tom Fallon, on the Ridge. There had been healing and comfort for her sore mind in that little interval of time with Tom there. She had come home feeling soothed and more at peace; there had been nothing wrong in their being there together.

And then she remembered his face tonight and the tone of his voice when that little word 'darling' had slipped out — The look in his eyes, naked and poignant and unashamed, the warmth and tenderness in his shaken voice that had been like a shining garment wrapped about her chilled body.

She caught her breath and her eyes went wide and frightened. What was this sudden sweet stirring in her heart? This warmth and tenderness that she had never known before? Could it be possible that she had fallen in love with Tom Fallon? Her mind cried out in shocked protest, but her heart said, "Yes, yes, yes — this is why you couldn't get excited about Larry! This is why you couldn't give up the farm, to go and live with Larry!"

"Oh, no — no — I won't have it like that! I won't be in love with him — I *won't*!" she wailed, deep in her frightened, stricken mind. But her heart went relentlessly on, "You didn't ask for it — but you can never deny it! He knows it, too — he feels as you do — you saw it in his eyes, heard it in his voice tonight. You love him and he loves you — and he has a wife who has a greater claim on him than if there were children."

She was bitterly ashamed, guilty; as

though she had deliberately tried to rob that pathetic, white-faced, golden-haired woman she had seen sitting up in bed, sobbing like a frightened child, the night Martha had hurt her ankle. That the whole emotional climax had crept up on her without warning seemed to her no excuse. No hope of forgiveness.

She remembered Tom again as he had stood in the kitchen looking down at her and calling her 'darling.' She had been startled and she had looked up at him swiftly, and he had said, "Yes, I called you 'darling' — " She broke off her thoughts with an effort and beat her hands soundlessly together, on the ragged edge of hysteria.

11

THE inquest was held the following afternoon, and it seemed that, except for the few bedridden in the town, everybody was there.

Everybody, that is, except Megan and her father. For contrary to Jim's uneasy fear, neither he nor Megan had been called to appear. Megan didn't quite know whether to be more relieved, or more frightened that neither she nor her father had received orders to appear.

At about four o'clock Laurence came down the road and turned in at the gate grinning at her warmly and happily.

"I came over with the coroner and some of the county officers," he told her cheerfully, dropping down on the steps at her feet and baring his head to the soft wind. "Pleasant Grove's certainly getting her name in the papers. There was a newspaper correspondent for one of the Atlanta papers at the inquest."

Megan asked, after a moment, "What — what did the inquest find — "

"Death by means of a sharp instrument at the hands of party or parties unknown," answered Laurence, looking up at her white, drawn face with surprise. "Oh look here, darling, I had no idea you were such a close friend of hers."

"I — wasn't, really," admitted Megan. "But — I knew her and — it's been a shock — "

"Of course," said Larry gently. He took her hand in his and held it closely. "We won't talk about it — "

"Yes!" said Megan so sharply that Laurence turned surprised eyes upon her. Megan managed a faint smile and said, "I — I really want to know — whatever they could learn — "

"Well, it wasn't much," said Laurence. "No trace of the weapon, a knife or a dagger of some sort. No trace of robbery or anything of that kind. Her purse was found with more than thirty dollars in it. They feel sure that if she had surprised a burglar at work, he would not have left the purse. They believe that she was killed by someone she knew — or at least, someone she was not afraid of. There were no signs of a struggle in the place."

Megan sat very still, her hands locked tightly in her lap.

Killed by someone she knew! Someone she was not afraid of!

"There was one sensation," said Laurence after a moment, not looking at Megan His eyes were on the garden, where, despite the fact that it was almost Christmas, a few late zinnias and marigolds were still in bloom and the chrysanthemums were great shaggy things of glowing beauty. "That was when the telegram from her husband arrived — "

Megan gasped and stared at him in complete amazement.

"Her — husband?" she repeated incredulously.

Laurence nodded. "That seemed as much of a shock to everybody there as it is to you," he told her. "But it seems that when the detectives were going through her papers yesterday they found that she had a husband she was separated from. He's flying east to claim the body. Should be here tomorrow or next day, they thought."

"But she was a widow!" Megan protested, dazedly.

"Apparently not," said Laurence, looking up as Annie appeared behind the screen door that led into the hall. "Hello, Annie — how about putting another plate on the table and letting me stay for supper?"

"Yes, Mister Larry — I'll be glad to," she assured him, beaming, and then asked uneasily, "Excuse me, but could I talk to you — for a few minutes?"

Laurence looked surprised, but got to his feet.

"Of course, Annie — don't tell me you want to divorce Amos, after all these years!" he laughed, excusing himself to Megan as he moved towards the screen door which Annie held open for him.

She was sitting in the living room. when Laurence came back from his talk with Annie. His brow was furrowed a little and he looked perplexed.

"That's the darndest story I ever heard," he admitted as he sat down opposite Megan and folded his arms across his chest. "I don't know what to make of it — but Annie's not the imaginative sort. She's always seemed so sensible and levelheaded, such good sound common sense — you wouldn't expect her to believe in ghosts, would you?"

Megan looked at him, bewildered, a little irritable by reason of the nerve strain under which she labored.

"What on earth are you talking about?" she asked.

"Annie's just been telling me a yarn — I told her that I'd have to go to Squire Etheridge and pass it on to him, because he's nominally in charge of the case here, though of course the bright boys from the county seat will want a share in it. But anyway, this is what Annie told me."

He leaned forward and looked at her straightly.

"I suppose you know about that little old family burying ground at the foot of the Ridge, just at the top of your pasture, west of your rock," he began.

Megan wrinkled her forehead a little. She remembered the place, of course. A small plot, probably twenty feet by twenty feet, enclosed by a rust-eaten iron fence, with a gate from which the padlock had long ago given way. Inside the rusty fence, there was a thick tangle of junglelike growth and a camellia bush that had grown almost into a tree. No names were on the several mounds enclosed, and no one knew to whose family the little plot belonged.

"Yes, I know the place, of course," Megan answered waiting tensely, little prickles of chill running up and down her spine like icy fingers.

"Well, it seems that Amos was coming home night before last a bit late. He was passing the little burying ground when suddenly he saw something that froze him in his tracks."

"You can't possibly mean that he thought he saw the usual wavering white figure — " Megan almost laughed.

Laurence nodded. "Nothing less," he told her solemnly. "It was, he claimed, at least eight feet tall and it didn't have any shape to it, just sort of like it was being poured, he expressed it. There was something shiny about it — the moon was not quite full but the light was good in the meadow. He says the ghost — he's quite sure, of course, that it was a ghost — floated along the meadow fence and then went towards the rusty iron fence. He says it moved inside the fence, and bent down above one of the old graves and hid something. And then it stood up, and looked around and moved back out of the fence and turned away from Amos — and Amos, recovering a little from his paralysis, made it home in practically nothing flat!"

Megan said uneasily, "He had probably been drinking some of that terrible 'white mule' his friends whip up — and he was seeing things!"

Laurence nodded. "That's the line I would follow, if it were not for the fact that that night, possibly a few minutes before Amos saw the eight-foot-high ghost, a woman had been killed and the weapon has not been found," he pointed out.

Megan said swiftly, "You can't possibly think that Amos' hallucination had anything to do with — with that?"

"I don't know, of course," Laurence answered. "But of course any unusual happening that night, at around that time, will have to be carefully investigated."

140

He hesitated a moment and then he said quietly, "There is no reason whatever, Megan, for anybody to know that you were on the Ridge with Fallon at the time Mrs. Stevenson was murdered."

And without waiting for her to recover from the shock of his quiet words and their implication, he went quietly out and the door closed behind him.

She sat there for a long time after he had gone. So Amos had seen her with Tom! And Amos had told Laurence.

She couldn't guess at what Laurence might be thinking. In the light of her own recent and appalling discovery that she was in love with Tom, she felt guilty and ashamed, as though in losing her heart to a man bound as Tom was, she had done some wicked and irretrievable thing. It was no good trying to remind herself that she had not asked for this, that it had slipped up on her secretly, so that she had had no forewarning, so that she had not been able to fight it.

She bent forward and put her face in her hands and was still — until a soft movement behind her startled her, and she straightened with a little jerk to find Annie in the doorway watching her with compassionate eyes.

"We didn' want to tell Mister Laurence, Miss Meggie — but we had to," said the gentle voice.

"Of course, Annie," she managed unsteadily. Megan heaved herself to her feet and went upstairs. She grimaced a little as she looked at herself in the mirror. She was white to the lips, there were shadows beneath her dark eyes, and her hair was untidy.

She showered and donned fresh things, a soft green jersey dress the shade of the first new green in spring that has almost a tinge of yellow in it. She brushed her hair until it gleamed and crackled beneath the vigorous onslaught of the brush. She rubbed a bit of rouge into her cheeks and applied lipstick carefully. When she had finished, the girl who looked back at her gave her a bit of badly needed courage for whatever ordeal might await her.

12

LAURENCE came back a little later, but he was not alone. With him was a stocky young man whose face looked that of a man in his early thirties, but whose hair was thickly streaked with gray. He had a pleasant, friendly manner, yet one felt instinctively that he could be tough should occasion require it.

Laurence performed the introductions, saying casually, "Meggie, this is Bob Reynolds. He's a detective from the county police who's looking into this business. Miss MacTavish, Mr. Reynolds."

"Hello," said Bob Reynolds with a friendly smile and a firm, pleasant handclasp. "This is quite a yarn your handyman's been spilling, Miss MacTavish I'd like to talk to him if I may."

"Of course," said Megan, looking uncertainly at Laurence. "Shall I call him in here — "

"I think Amos would be more at ease if we talked to him outside, Bob. Meggie — suppose I show Bob the way?" suggested Laurence.

It was close to thirty minutes before they returned, and as they came along the hall, Megan heard their lowpitched, cautious voices and her nerves crisped a little. But by the time they reached the living room, she had herself well in hand, and could face them with a degree of composure that passed muster in Bob Reynolds' eyes, though she thought Laurence gave her a swift, almost warning glance.

"What would be *your* explanation for Amos' story, Miss MacTavish? How would you account for it?" Bob asked.

Megan set her teeth hard for a moment and there was pure panic in her eyes, but before she could say anything Bob went on quickly, "I mean, of course, that you are quite familiar with the surrounding territory — it's all strange to me. Do you know of anything that could have alarmed Amos so that he would have mistaken it for an eight-foot ghost?"

"I've been trying to think," Megan said thoughtfully. "There are some old fruit trees around that place. Pear trees in full bloom look ghostly in the dark — only it's too early for them to be blooming. I can't remember whether the trunks of any of the trees have been whitewashed lately."

Bob nodded, his eyes intent. "A tree trunk white-washed half way up, *is* a rather spooky looking thing in the dark. Still, Amos is so sure that the 'spook' went inside the gate and bent above one of the old mounds — " He broke off, grinned and said briskly, "Oh well, we'll have to wait for daylight to make an intensive search of the place, I suppose. From the description Amos and Larry both have given me, I don't imagine we could accomplish much by searching tonight. I'll be over first thing in the morning, and we'll give the place a going over."

He was obviously on the verge of leaving and Megan said quickly, "Won't you stay for supper, Mr. Reynolds? We'd like having you!"

"Better take her up on that, Bob. Annie's the best cook in seven states — at a conservative estimate!" said Laurence lightly.

Bob beamed happily, "Well now, if you're sure it won't be an imposition, there's nothing I'd like better!" he assured Megan gratefully. "And I'll give you a lift back to Meadersville later, Larry."

"Swell!" Laurence agreed happily.

Just as Annie came to the door to announce that supper was ready, the front door opened and Jim came in. Megan caught a glimpse of him before Laurence or Bob saw him: he looked desperately tired and forlorn, his shoulders drooping. But the next moment he became aware of the stranger in the living room. His shoulders went back and his head went up, and he came in, bracing himself, friendly, polite, hospitable, as Laurence performed the introductions.

Annie made her delayed announcement of supper, and they went in and were seated, before Jim spoke to Bob. "So you are investigating our — tragedy, Mr. Reynolds?"

"Yes," answered Bob, eyeing hungrily the crisply browned stuffed chicken that Annie had placed before Jim, who was about to wield an expert carving knife. "Let's not talk about it now. After all, a meal like this deserves more cheerful and appreciative table conversation!"

When the meal was over, and the men were settled in the living room, Megan stayed to help Annie clear the table. And while she was thus engaged, Laurence came back into the dining room, and stood at her shoulder and said very low, "I just wanted you to know, Meggie, that — everything is quite all right. There's nothing at all for you to worry about."

Megan looked up at him, tears thick in her eyes, her mouth tremulous. "I — met him by accident, Larry. I didn't plan it — *truly*."

He looked down at her, frowning.

"But — good heavens, Meggie, don't you suppose I know that?" he protested, almost as though he resented her feeling that she should offer such an explanation.

She caught her breath and a wave of relief swept over her. She smiled through her tears and said huskily, "Thanks, Larry."

"For what?" The frown still drew his brows together. "For Heaven's sake, Meggie — I've known you since you were a baby — don't you suppose I know you well enough to know that if you met Tom Fallon on the Ridge at midnight, it was an accidental meeting?"

Her smile grew deeper, and she blinked the tears from her eyes and said once more, gratefully, "Thanks, dear! Thanks!"

Laurence hesitated a moment and then he said quietly, "I'd like to ask you something, Meggie — mind?"

"No, of course not."

"Then — are you in love with Fallon?"

The words were quietly spoken, but they took her breath so that she could only look up at him, unable to speak. But the way the color flowed into her face, the look in her eyes gave him all the answer he needed.

"So that's why you — couldn't get excited about marrying me," he said after a moment, very quietly.

She set her teeth hard in her lower lip, not daring to trust her voice to answer him, and after a little he said in a tone of the greatest gentleness, "Poor little Meggie! Always doing things the hard way."

By now she had steadied her voice, and she faced him straightly. "If — you'll j-j-just give me a little time, Larry — " she managed.

His brows were drawn deep now in

a frown and his look was puzzled. "A little time, Meggie?" he repeated. "For what?"

"To pull myself together and get over this — this — craziness about — about Tom," she said. "Because I will, you know. I'll — I'll get over it and — maybe if you haven't got disgusted with me before that — "

"Oh, I'll be around, Meggie. Is that what you mean?" asked Larry, and now there was a grimness in his voice, a coldness in his eyes that chilled her a little. "You are the only girl for me. You've always been. I'm a slow and plodding cuss, but once I get my mind — and my heart — made up, I hold on. But what makes you so sure that you can get over what you feel for Fallon?"

"Because I'm *going* to!" she told him with determination.

Laurence laughed. But it was an entirely mirthless laugh and his hand on her shoulder was gentle, compassionate.

"Poor little Meggie!" he said as

151

though she had been about five years old and not very bright. "You still think you have anything to say about such things?"

"I'll get over it — or never be able to live with myself again!" she told him steadily.

Laurence nodded. "Then I can feel a little encouraged. Because if you think for so much as a moment that you can end such a feeling — then it's not love!" he said.

He turned away from her then as Bob called to him from the hall, and a little later they were gone.

Megan and her father sat in the living room for a little in silence after they had gone. It was Jim who finally broke the silence.

"Did you know that she — was married?" he asked heavily.

"Yes," Megan nodded. "Laurence told me."

Jim's face twisted. "What a laugh she must have got out of me — wanting to marry her. And she told me she would — she never for a moment even hinted that she was not a widow!"

Megan waited, knowing a little of the release that would come to him if he could rid his mind of these revelations.

"I suppose she got a kick out of making a fool of me," he broke off and passed a hand across his eyes and looked straight at Megan. "But I didn't kill her," he finished quietly, with a simple dignity that was somehow oddly touching.

"I know you didn't, dear," Megan assured him swiftly.

He studied her for a moment and then he asked in a puzzled tone, "Meggie, how did you and I start disliking each other? I've been doing a good deal of thinking lately. I admire you very much. You're a fine girl and a brave girl, and — well, I can't quite understand why it is that we seem to rub each other the wrong way all the time."

"I don't either, Dad," Megan

admitted, touched in spite of herself by the way he had said humbly, 'I was lonely.' "I've always admired you too — but I guess I used to side with Mother when you two disagreed, and — somehow, I just gradually got into taking sides against you."

"Which of course was no secret to me, so I took the opposite, regardless of where you stood." Jim smiled and looked more like his old casual, mocking self. "I'll probably be just as hard to get along with tomorrow, as I was yesterday — only tonight, I'm — well, I'm lonely, Meggie, and tired, and maybe — just a little afraid. Could we be friends, do you suppose?"

"Of course, Dad!" She bent swiftly and kissed his cheek.

Jim looked at her for a moment and then nodded as though he had reached some sort of decision.

"The whole thing, of course," he said, "boils down to the fact that I've been jealous of you since the day you were born."

"Jealous, Dad?" the astonished Megan repeated.

He nodded. "I adored your mother, Meggie. I know now that it was a jealous, possessive love, the sort of thing that makes a spoiled little boy say 'if we can't play *my* way, then I won't play at all.' We were happy at first. I was first with her; her every thought was for me, for my comfort, my happiness, my well being. And then — you came along, and took up a lot of your mother's tenderness and thought, and I had to take second place. And like the no-good I was, I resented it."

Megan shuddered, walking down the long halls of memory, seeing her mother in tears, bitterly hurt by some caustic word, some calculatedly cruel act of her father's.

"Oh but, Dad — that's — why, that's wicked! Poor Mother!" she said just above her breath. "It wasn't that she loved me more than she loved you; it was that I *needed* her more."

"And I resented that, too!" said her

father. "Odd, what a chastening effect it has on a man, when he realizes that he has made a fool of himself!" he said at last. "I feel as though I'd been kicked."

"But it's all over and done with, Dad — we can have a lot of fun together — " Megan began eagerly.

"Over and done with, Meggie? Don't kid yourself, my dear — we haven't seen the last of this! Nor heard it, either," he corrected her swiftly. "Had you realized that if Amos was on the Ridge that night, as he must have been to tell Larry the story he did, the chances are excellent that he saw you — as well as the eight-foot-tall ghost?"

Megan nodded, her face white but her outward composure commendable. "I know that he did, Dad," she said quietly. "He told Larry."

Her father's body jerked like a marionette on a string manipulated by an inexpert puppeteer.

"Told Larry — that you were on

the Ridge with Fallon?" he repeated sharply.

Megan nodded.

For a moment Jim was very still, like a man suddenly paralyzed. And then very carefully he asked, "Did he tell that fellow Reynolds?"

Megan shook her head, her hands cold in her lap.

"He — didn't seem to think it was necessary," she managed the words with difficulty. "He seemed to think that the fact that I *was* there gave me an alibi. If I was there at that time, I couldn't possibly have been across the road — even if I had had a motive."

Her father smiled, a mirthless smile that made him look suddenly very old and very tired. "Now if only somebody had seen me going for my walk — "

"Perhaps somebody did," said Megan eagerly.

He shook his head. "I saw no one — after I left Alicia," he said quietly and distinctly.

She stiffened a little and her eyes were wide.

"You — saw her — that night?" she whispered, her lips pallid.

"At eleven-thirty," said Jim and heaved a sigh as he ran his fingers through his magnificent crop of silvery-gray hair. "The way I figure it, she couldn't have been alone, after I left her, more than ten or fifteen minutes."

His fingers trembled a little as he filled his handsome pipe and tamped the tobacco carefully into the mellow bowl, but his eyes did not leave Megan's white, frightened face.

"We quarrelled," said Jim quietly, distinctly, "when she admitted that she had not the slightest idea of marrying me. She called me a pompous old fool and a lot of equally uncomplimentary things. But I didn't kill her, Megan, I swear it."

Suddenly Megan was on her knees beside him, her arms close about him, her cheek hard against his, all the ugliness and the animosity that had colored their relations for years wiped out between them in this moment when she ached with pity for him, and when for the first time in her adult life she had begun to have some glimmering of understanding him.

"But you didn't — you *couldn't* — have done it, Dad! Nobody could ever make me believe you did!" she comforted him, as though he had been the child, she the parent.

13

IT was long before she slept that
night, but in spite of the unpleasant
turmoil and excitement of the last
forty-eight hours, she was more at
peace than she had been in a long
time.

She had finished her morning chores,
and was busy with a seed catalog and
an order blank when Laurence arrived
with Bob Reynolds.

"We found something that proves
that Amos was telling us the truth
— that is, that he *did* see something
at the old burying ground that night,"
said Laurence quickly.

"We found a knife," he answered
the look of questioning in her eyes,
and Megan caught her breath and
went white as the collar of her trim
morning frock. "Bob feels sure it is
— the knife."

160

She did not speak, but her eyes pleaded with him and Laurence went on quietly, "There's not much possibility of fingerprints. The knife was buried halfway up the hilt, and it rained later on that night, and of course, the dews are very heavy this time of the year. It was just an ordinary kitchen knife, such as any hardware store sells by the gross every year — probably every kitchen in Pleasant Grove has one or two exactly like it."

Megan was conscious that she was breathing a little more easily. She said hurriedly, lest Laurence should notice that, "Then — you aren't much better off than you were before so far as identification."

Annie appeared at the door behind him, unobtrusive, yet obviously excited. Her voice was high as she answered Megan's questioning look. "Mister Fallon's sister is here, Miss Meggie."

Megan caught her breath and felt as though every drop of blood in her body had congealed about her heart. Her eyes were wide and frightened, and she was suddenly conscious that Bob Reynolds was watching her narrowly, an odd light in his eyes.

"Of course, Annie, I'll see her," she made herself say swiftly, steadying her voice with an effort. "If you'll excuse — ?"

But Bob Reynolds said casually, with a look in his eyes that was not at all casual, "Why not see her in here, Miss MacTavish?"

Megan looked sharply at him and said instantly, "But why? It's no doubt a personal matter — I mean it can't possibly have any connection — " But beneath the look in his eyes her voice broke.

"Of course not," Bob agreed amiably, but still with that wary look in his eyes. "But just the same — "

And behind Annie, Megan saw, with a feeling of shock, Martha Evans, short, stocky, commonplace looking. Her neat dark percale dress and the smoothness of her hair that was streaked with gray only emphasized the look of barely restrained terror in her eyes.

Miss Martha nodded to Megan and addressed herself to Bob, after giving Laurence a steady, straight look.

"You're the detective-fellow?" she asked Bob curtly.

"Yes, Miss Fallon — my name's Reynolds," answered Bob.

Martha nodded and said, "Well, my name's not Fallon. I'm Tom Fallon's sister-in-law, not his sister. My name's Evans — Martha Evans."

Laurence unobtrusively turned a chair towards her and she nodded her thanks and sank into it with a movement that was almost of collapse, as though her knees were shaking violently, and she was very glad of the support the chair gave her.

"So you found it," she said when she had drawn a deep hard breath and Megan, sick with pity and bewilderment, saw the work-roughened hands gripped so tightly together that the knuckles were small white mounds.

163

Bob said gently, "Found what, Miss Evans?"

She looked up at him so sharply that the sunlight fell harshly on the round lenses of her old-fashioned spectacles and she made a sound that was half a snort, half a sniff of contempt.

"The knife, of course," she answered him curtly.

Bob made a short, swiftly controlled movement, but his face was guarded, so that only if you had been watching him closely could you have noted that involuntary start of surprise.

"Suppose you tell us about the knife, Miss Evans," he said gently.

Martha nodded. "What else do you think I came here for?" she sniffed, and abruptly she added, "Only — the Stevenson woman wasn't killed with that knife, young man."

"No?" asked Bob very gently, very politely, almost as though his interest had been too casual to make the statement of any importance.

"No!" the word came explosively.

"Then why was it necessary to hide it so — er — melodramatically?" wondered Bob aloud.

Martha breathed deeply and with difficulty.

"Because," she told him — and Megan's eyes were thick with tears for the stark agony that shone so clearly in the tired, faded eyes behind those old-fashioned spectacles — "because — my sister is a — a mental case," she managed at last.

Bob waited.

Laurence was very still, watching Martha, his arms folded across his chest, leaning against the big old-fashioned rolltop desk where Megan kept her accounts and books.

"You mean," said Bob, after a moment designed to give Martha a respite so that she could breathe again, "that your sister was not accountable for her actions — "

"I mean, young man, that my sister — had periods of lucidity," she said harshly. "But Tom thought, poor soul,

165

that she was getting better — that there was hope for her. But I didn't deceive myself. Even if I had wanted to — her attack on me one night — "

Her voice broke and her face worked convulsively, but she did not lower her head, nor make any effort to hide her face from them.

Megan said quietly, "The night you fell and hurt your ankle?"

Martha said huskily, "Only I didn't fall — she pushed me down the steps."

Bob waited, and after a little, she went on huskily, "Tom and I saw to it that there was never any — any instrument around that she could use to hurt herself — or anybody else. Tom thought she was bedridden; I hadn't told him that she was growing stronger, that she could walk — not very far, but at least she was no longer helpless. I knew, of course, the danger that was growing around her — danger that she might slip away from me and — do some horrible thing — "

Bob said swiftly, "Then you mean

that she managed to get away and kill Mrs. Stevenson?"

Martha flung up her head. Her eyes blazed.

"She did nothing of the sort! Use your head, young man. It's a mile from our house to Mrs. Stevenson's place — she couldn't travel that far. And she hasn't been out of my sight one single minute since the night she attacked me," she blazed at him hotly.

Bob said gently, "We have only your word for that, Miss Evans."

Martha's stocky body slumped a little and she said wearily, "Yes, of course — you have only my word for it — "

"And the knife, Miss Evans?" asked Bob very quietly.

She seemed to wince as though he had struck her. She drew a deep breath and lifted her head a little, though her shoulders sagged.

"Yes, the knife," she repeated. "That was — night before last. As I said, Tom didn't know that Letty could get out of bed, or walk; he thought it was a little foolish of me to keep every sharp-pointed instrument in the house under lock and key. He thought as long as we kept them out of her room, out of her reach — " She shrugged tiredly and then she went on in that heavy, exhausted voice, "so he left a knife out on the kitchen sink night before last. I'd — had a good deal of trouble with Letty and I was very tired. I slept in her room, and I thought that she was sleeping soundly, and so I let myself go to sleep. When I woke up — I don't know what woke me, but — suddenly I was wide-awake, and — there was Letty standing beside my bed, bending over me, the moonlight on — that knife in her hand. I screamed, and that roused Tom, and — well, between us we managed to get the knife away from her. She fought hard, and then suddenly — she went to pieces, just slumped between us like a ragdoll that's lost all its sawdust. We got her to bed. We knew there was nothing we could do for her. The doctor had warned us — any sudden exertion, excitement — would almost certainly result in a brain hemorrhage — " She paused again and then went on, "I left her with Tom. I wanted to get rid of that awful knife, once and for all time. So I hid it — where you found it."

She was limp with exhaustion and nerve strain and Bob let her rest for a moment before he asked very gently, "And — your sister, Miss Evans?"

Martha said in a voice that was a ghost of sound, "She — died early this morning."

14

IT was an hour later, after Martha had had a cup of coffee and a chance to rest a little, that Bob went over the story of the hiding of the knife again.

"It seems quite a coincidence, Miss Evans, that all this happened the same night that Mrs. Stevenson was killed," he pointed out.

"I don't know anything about that, young man," said Martha with the faintest possible trace of her old brusqueness. "All I know is that when I heard you'd found the knife, I was afraid some innocent person would be accused of doing away with the Stevenson woman by means of that knife. And I knew I had to come and tell you about it, since telling you couldn't cause my poor little Letty any trouble — now."

Bob nodded, sitting on the edge of the desk, his eyes fastened on Martha's face.

"Amos, who saw the knife being hidden, spoke of a 'thing in white, about eight feet tall' — " he mentioned.

There was the faintest possible trace of a smile in Martha's tired eyes.

"I know," she told him quietly. "It was a bright moonlight night and you never know who may be roaming around late at night in these parts," and for just the barest instant her glance flickered towards Megan and away. "I didn't want anyone to see me — you can understand that, of course. And it occurred to me that that old place would be an ideal place to hide something you didn't ever want found. But if somebody saw me — and recognized me — you see?"

Bob nodded. "Of course," he answered quickly.

"Well, Tom was with Letty," Martha went on. "I slipped out into the kitchen, got the knife, and took a sheet out of the

171

linen closet. I also put one of Tom's hats on the end of a walking stick, and held the stick above my head, under the sheet I imagine I must have looked pretty fearsome. But you see, I wanted anybody who saw me to think that he was seeing a ghost — and if such things as ghosts exist, surely their favorite place would be something like that old overgrown garden. I never dreamed that anybody seeing me would stop long enough to see what I was doing — or, if he did, that he would report it to anybody."

"You didn't see Amos?" asked Bob quickly.

"No," answered Martha, and hesitated so oddly that Bob's attention caught and grew stronger.

"Who did you see then?" demanded Bob.

"No one," answered Martha firmly. Too firmly. Too emphatically. "I saw no one at all — no one."

Bob said sternly, "You're not telling me the truth, Miss Evans. Up to now,

I believe you. But if you start telling me lies now, don't you see you're likely to make me believe that all you've told me is a lie!"

Martha said grimly, "You can believe anything you want to, young man. I've told you all I'm going to tell you."

She got up and Bob said sternly, "I've not finished yet — "

Martha eyed him as though he had been an importunate beggar, and said coolly, "Haven't you? Well, I have. Good day to you all."

She looked at Megan and said tonelessly, "Tom and I are — taking Letty home. We're leaving today, so this will be good-bye — and — thanks for all you've done."

"Martha, whom did you see that night?" Bob demanded sharply. "I can forbid you to leave, you know — I can hold you as a material witness — "

"A witness to what? I wasn't within a mile of the Stevenson place," Miss Martha pointed out. "Amos is my alibi, just as I am his. I'd say that he and

I are the two people who couldn't possibly have had anything to do with the murder."

"But you did see someone that night — " began Bob.

She met his eyes straightly and said coolly, "Did I?"

Megan drew a deep breath and said levelly, "You saw me, didn't you, Martha?"

Bob flung her a startled glance, but Laurence's mouth only tightened a little.

Martha looked straight at Megan and then she sighed and nodded. "Yes, I saw you," she admitted.

Bob said quickly, "Look here, Miss MacTavish, you haven't told me anything about being up there that night — "

Bob was frowning at Megan, all friendliness and liking gone from his face. "Who was with you?" he asked sternly. "Don't tell me you went out alone at that time of night."

Megan said quietly, "No, I wasn't

alone. I was when I left the house. But when I reached the Ridge — Mr. Fallon was there and we talked a little while."

"Oh," said Bob in a peculiar tone that made Martha bristle. "So Mr. Fallon was on the Ridge — at the same time that Miss Evans here says he was helping her to take care of his wife — "

Martha made a clumsy gesture and sighed.

"Oh well, Megan, if you're determined to see your reputation blown higher than a kite, there's nothing I can do to stop you," she said wearily. "I lied about Tom being in the house when I woke up and found my sister with the knife. I thought he was. I'd heard him go to his room and I hadn't heard him leave it. But when I woke up and screamed, he didn't answer me. I had my hands full with — my poor Letty. But when I finally got her quiet — when she — collapsed, I knew Tom wasn't in the house. He likes to walk at night. He is cooped up all day in the school, so he often goes for long walks. When I got my sister to bed, and knew that she would be quiet for some time, I locked her in and went out. Then as I was coming back I saw Tom coming down from the Ridge. And when I looked down over the meadow, I saw Megan going towards the MacTavish place. But I couldn't see that it would help any, if I told it — "

Bob was watching Megan curiously, a queer look in his eyes. He said coldly, "All right, Miss MacTavish — let's hear your story."

Megan said huskily, "There's no story. I was restless and couldn't sleep. The walk up to the Ridge is a favorite of mine and I often go there. It was quite by accident that I met Mr. Fallon there, and we talked, probably not more than ten or fifteen minutes. That's all."

Bob was angry and made no pretense of concealing it.

"Yet you couldn't bring yourself to

tell me about this until it was literally forced out of you. Don't you see how that looks, Miss MacTavish?"

There was a taut moment of silence. In that silence Megan felt that she could almost hear the hard, uneven pounding of her heart, and she had a crazy feeling that the others must surely hear it, too — and wonder about it.

Bob lit a cigarette, first securing permission from Megan and Martha, and lighting it very carefully, his eyes centered on the tiny flame of the match until the cigarette was burning evenly and smoothly. He took it out of his mouth and for a moment regarded the tip of it as though with absorbed interest.

And then he looked at Miss Martha and said very gently, "Miss Evans, just why did you kill Mrs. Stevenson?"

It was so unexpected, and the tone of his quiet, even voice was in such contrast to the thing he said that for a moment everybody in the room went rigid; and outside the door, in the shadowy hall, there was a smothered gasp from the unseen, but listening Annie.

Martha drew a hard breath and lifted her hands in a little gesture of helplessness before she gripped them once more about the arms of her chair. She moistened dry lips and after a moment she said, her voice so colorless and so low that they had to strain their ears to hear at all. "I — I hated her. She was a wicked woman. She made so much trouble for everybody. She had started spreading lies and slander about Tom."

The tired voice died and she opened her eyes and looked at Megan and said faintly, "I'm sorry, but I might as well tell the whole story. This young man seems to be able to find out a lot of things."

"There's no reason why you shouldn't tell it all," said Laurence gently. "There was nothing wrong in Fallon's friendship with Megan."

Bob was watching Laurence with

a curiously intent look in his eyes. Laurence met his gaze almost belligerently and the dark color deepened a little in his face. Bob grinned and turned back to Martha.

"So Mrs. Stevenson was broadcasting the fact that Miss MacTavish and Mr. Fallon were friends, and hinting that there was more to it than that, and you decided to have a talk with her — was that it?" his gentle voice asked.

She rubbed her hands together as though the palms were damp and her voice steadied a little. "Yes, that was it," she said evenly. "And Mrs. Stevenson was curious about Letty's illness and she came prying and snooping. Tom and I knew that if the people here in Pleasant Grove knew that Letty was — of unsound mind, they might be afraid of her, for all that she was completely helpless, and that Tom might lose his job, or worse still, that he might be forced to — put Letty away in an — institution."

"So you went to have a talk with Mrs.

Stevenson," Bob prompted Martha, his tone gentle and friendly.

"Yes," said Martha, and now she was pleating the crisp percale of her housedress over her knee with twitching fingers, her eyes on the task. "There's a short cut through the woods, and it isn't far. I got my sister to bed and to sleep. As I've already told you, Tom was out of the house. I found Mrs. Stevenson was not alone. I waited — "

"She wasn't alone?" Bob jerked her up sharply.

Martha shook her head.

"Mr. MacTavish was with her," she said, and now Megan held her breath and her teeth were clenched. "He left a few minutes after I got there.

"I waited until he had gone," Martha went on wearily. "Then I knocked and she opened the door. She was surprised to see me, and not very — pleasant. I tried to tell her why I had come, but she only laughed. She said that there must be a lot of truth in the stories about Tom and Megan or he and I would not have been so alarmed — and she added that she knew that Letty was — out of her mind — and that she was a menace to the neighborhood. She said she intended to start a movement to have her — committed — " Her voice broke, and after a superhuman effort at control, she said thinly, "And so — I killed her."

It was once more Bob who broke the tense, breathless pause. He scrubbed out the glowing tip of his cigarette as he spoke, his eyes on the crushed cigarette in the old glass ashtray, his voice very quiet and gentle, "The truth is, Miss Evans, that your sister, not you, killed Mrs. Stevenson."

The room was stunned, incredulous. Megan looked, appalled at the devastation that swept over Martha's face before she huddled back in her chair, put her hands over her face and moaned like a stricken animal. There could be no doubt that Bob had hit upon the truth, that the valiant attempt Martha

Evans had made to shield the memory of her sister was of no avail.

Bob sighed. He ran his hands through his hair and stood up, white and tired, haggard almost, as though the long scene had been almost as much of an ordeal for him as for the broken, suddenly old woman before them.

15

"BUT how could you possibly know — " Megan demanded of Bob.

It was late in the afternoon of an extremely hectic day after all the loose ends and the final details of the tragic story had been cleared up. Martha and Tom had departed on their sad errand of 'taking Letty home' to lie beside the little son who had never lived.

Megan had asked Bob and Laurence to stay for supper and they had accepted gratefully. And now they were in the living room, with Jim listening and looking on, withdrawn and pale, but genial and pleasant when spoken to. In the kitchen Annie was going methodically about the job of getting supper ready and now and then her low-toned comments, and Amos' equally cautious rejoinders could be heard as a sort of murmur, the words indistinguishable.

"I didn't know, of course," Bob answered frankly. "It was just that — well, call it a hunch, what you will. That story was a bit too elaborate for the mere hiding of a knife with which an insane person might harm a member of the family."

"I thought of that, too, of course," Laurence contributed.

"Then when she began to talk about going to Mrs. Stevenson's — remember she mentioned the short cut through the woods? Yet she had been at some pains to assure us that her sister's strength was not sufficient for her to walk to the Stevenson place. But if there was a short cut through the woods, and if her sister had followed her and overheard her quarrel with the Stevenson woman, and the sister had been frightened, excited, as she most certainly would have been — do you see?"

"Poor Martha!" said Megan huskily.

Her mouth quivered and there were tears in her eyes.

Laurence looked at her swiftly and said quietly, "And poor Tom Fallon!"

Megan felt her cheeks grow warm, but she met his eyes straightly and it was Laurence who turned away.

"And now," said Bob squaring his shoulders, "let's talk about something else, shall we? This case — well, it's sort of got me down. I don't like pursuing pitiful old women and digging out their tragic, terrible secrets."

"An excellent idea," said Jim heartily. He asked a question about politics and a moment later he and Bob were off in an argument that it was obvious they both enjoyed.

Megan slipped away to the backyard to a big old rough bench beneath a live oak tree and sat down, her head back, breathing deep of the crisp night air.

The night was very still, save for the faint shouts of children playing somewhere along the highway; behind her in the barn she heard the rustling of the cows as they settled themselves down for the night. The whole scene was quiet and calm and peaceful. So peaceful that it was hard to believe the horror and tragedy and terror that had gripped the place so short a time before.

She couldn't bear to think of Tom any more. She wouldn't let herself, and she was glad when she saw Laurence coming towards her across the dusky dooryard.

Megan started to rise, but he put his hand on her shoulder and pressed her back on the bench and said, "Your father and Bob are having the time of their lives. Bob's trying to give your father a satisfactory explanation as to why a born-and-bred Southerner is going to vote a Republican ticket. From the sound of things, they could go at it all night. They'll never miss us."

Megan relaxed a little. He lit a cigarette and they sat for a little companionably in silence.

"It's all — like a terrible dream," she

said huskily, and Laurence nodded.

"But you've waked up now, Megan, and sensible people don't brood over bad dreams or let them affect their future lives!" he reminded her almost sternly. "There's one thing out of the bad dream that you can remember, though — Fallon is free. After a decent interval of time — " He broke off and his hand made a little white gesture in the darkness.

Megan caught her breath and looked at him in surprise.

"I didn't mean that — after all, aren't you taking rather a lot for granted?" she protested heatedly. "Tom Fallon and I were — friends — "

"Tom Fallon was — and is — in love with you, and you know it," Laurence told her bluntly. "And besides, have you forgotten that you told me yourself you were in love with him?"

"I — I guess I am," she admitted humbly.

"You guess you are!" Laurence was caustic.

"Well, what I meant was — I'm all mixed up and confused — it's been so horrible — " she stammered faintly.

"That's understandable," Laurence conceded grudgingly. "But after awhile, you'll pull yourself together and be able to see clearly — and in a year or so — "

Annie's voice from the kitchen door announcing supper was the most welcome sound Megan had ever heard in all her life, and she rose so swiftly that Laurence's mouth tightened a little and his eyes were cold and hard as he followed her across the yard to the kitchen and into the dining room. Bob and Jim, still arguing furiously, were already waiting there.

During the meal, the argument, which both men were obviously enjoying, continued, making any attempt at conversation between Laurence and Megan no longer necessary for which she was heartily glad.

Later, Laurence and Megan said goodnight quite casually in the living room. After they had gone, Jim looked curiously at Megan, started to say something, and then was silent.

Megan was grateful for his restraint and said goodnight to him as briefly as she could. Tonight she was overwrought and her emotions were so tangled that she felt she would scream if one more word were spoken.

But fortunately for her peace of mind, there is always a great deal of work to be done on a farm, work that requires one's mind as well as one's body.

On the day after New Year's, Megan, together with farmers in the section, began to plow and plant and plan for the coming spring crop. She drove the big tractor, and her father tried honestly if clumsily to help. She and Amos and such day-by-day labor as they could acquire plowed and seeded the big open fields, turning back the rich, loamy dark earth; and Megan thrilled, as she always did, to the ever recurring miracle of dark, rich earth, of tiny seeds, and of food and clothing that were created by that miracle.

Healthily tired at the end of the day, sleeping soundly at night, her mind occupied with the coming of each day with the tasks that always seemed greater than the amount of time that could be given them, she discovered as week followed week, that the memories were fading.

She cut and packed gladioli for shipment to wholesale flower markets in the North. There were vegetable plants to be packed and shipped, too; rows of tender, feathery, green broccoli plants, peppers, onions, tomatoes.

She was grateful to Jim for his honest, if bungling attempts to help her. She tried not to let him know that his hands were clumsy with the delicate, fragile plants that he tried to pack; she managed to be the one to cut the tall green gladioli, which must be cut and packed for shipment just when the tiny beads of color began to appear at the ends of the green buds.

She knew he was bored, and that he resented the hard, back-breaking labor that it takes to run a farm effectively. She was always glad when he could be the one to drive the little old truck, heavily laden with packaged shipments, to Meadersville.

He came back from such a trip late one afternoon, his eyes shining with excitement, obviously with news that he considered of great importance.

It was already dusk, and the darkness had driven Megan in from the fields. She had shed her earth-stained dungarees, had a shower and was dressed for supper, busy in the kitchen helping Annie with the last duties of getting the meal on the table, when Jim came hurrying in.

He threw the express receipts for the larger shipments on the table and said excitedly, "The most marvelous thing has happened, Meggie — I've been offered a splendid opportunity! You know the county newspaper in Meadersville? The *Sentinel*?" demanded

Jim, as eager and excited as a boy. "Dick Morgan publishes it; he wants to hire me. What I'll have to do is write the editorials, and what news I can pick up. Mostly, right now, it comes from a wire service. Of course, the salary is really laughable — but I get a share of the profits and all that."

"It *is* wonderful, Dad, and of course you can do it!"

Megan assured him, sincerely. "I'm terribly proud of you. I'll bet there isn't another man in the whole county who has read as much, or studied as much of current events as you have."

By the time supper was on the table, and they were eating, he had launched excitedly into his plans, ambitious, slightly bombastic perhaps, for what he was going to do for the paper. Megan wondered why she had never before seen her father as he really was, like a small boy anxious for public approval and applause. If she was not too optimistic as to how long his enthusiasm would last, she could at least be glad he was happy now and busily planning.

When supper was over he broke off to say hesitantly, "Of course, Meggie, I know I promised to help you with the farm this year — but I hate to turn down a chance like this. A chance to — well, to be somebody important, and to have people listen to my views."

"Now don't you worry about the farm, or me," Megan assured him firmly. She did not even think of reminding him of the years when she had managed and worked the place, not only without his assistance, but with the actual added burden of his antagonism, his anxiety to get rid of the place.

Suddenly Jim said, "Oh, yes, I knew there was something I had forgotten. I saw Laurence while I was in town."

Megan looked up, feeling her father's eyes upon her and knew, by the sudden warmth of her face, that she was blushing. Which, she told herself furiously, was pretty silly, anyway you looked at it.

"He asked about you," said Jim, when she did not speak. "I asked him why we hadn't seen him lately, and he said he'd been pretty busy." Jim nodded. "Well, anyway, he said he'd be out soon, and sent you his love."

And Megan, a little warm something stirring in her heart, bent her head, and a tiny, secret smile touched her mouth for a moment.

16

THE busy, crowded days of spring melted into the even days of early summer and the crops stood lush and green in the fields, but Laurence did not come.

Megan was busy, working hard, and Jim was finding the newspaper business exciting, though he quarreled with Mr. Morgan occasionally. But his editorials had been well received; he was newly important in the community.

On a late June evening, when the whole world seemed locked in a golden haze of loveliness, Megan came up from the fields, intent on nothing more exciting than a brisk shower and fresh clothes, when she saw a car standing at the gate.

She came on into the kitchen and said, "Have we got company, Annie?"

"You better go see for yourself,

Miss Meggie," answered Annie in that colorless, careful voice.

Megan stripped the gaily figured scarf from her head, shook out her tumbled curls, and walked into the living room. The man who stood at the window turned to face her — and Megan was still, rigid with shock. Because the man who faced her was — Tom Fallon.

He had aged, and his face was set and grim, his eyes those of the tragically lost. But as he looked at her, some of the haggard look vanished from his face and he said in a tone just above a whisper, "You're lovelier than ever. I must apologize for coming back now, but I felt I had to see you before making a certain decision. Because — in a way, the decision concerns you. I mean — it is only fair that you should have the deciding voice."

Bewildered, Megan sat down, because her knees were shaking a little and she dared not trust them to hold her up any longer.

"Please sit down," she said, her voice

choked, "and — tell me all about it. How could I possibly have any part in the decision you are to make?"

His face hardened a little as though the implication of her words was hard to take. But he said quietly, "I've been offered the job of principal at the school again this year."

Megan caught her breath.

"But — but surely — you wouldn't want to come back — *here*?" she gasped.

"Let's not beat about the bush and tell polite lies, Megan," he said with a forthrightness that was rather staggering. "I know that it will be a long time before I can — speak to you of love, Megan. It would be the worst possible taste for me to do so now. But there was an evening, Megan, when we spoke our hearts — for the briefest possible moment. I haven't forgotten. Have you?"

Megan felt the color rush to her face and she could not quite meet his eyes. And she did not know that her mouth curled ever so little with the faintest possible expression of distaste.

"I — think that we were both a little — crazy that night," she told him, painfully. "It — it was — well, it didn't mean anything — " She stopped because his face, that could not grow any grayer or more tired, seemed to harden as though never again would it be mere flesh and blood and bones.

"So it's like that," he said very quietly, his tone tired and heavy and old. "I should have known that I was just seeing something that didn't really exist. You were emotionally upset and you were sorry for me — was that it, Megan?"

Megan sat very still. Because that was it. She knew it now.

She had imagined herself in love with Tom, because she had been caught by pity for his unhappy plight, and she had let herself be deceived into thinking that her pity for him was a stronger, more vital emotion. But now she saw clearly, in the light of the past few months' clarity of vision and peace of mind.

Tom stood up and said quietly, "Well, that's that. I didn't have a great deal of hope, of course. Maybe the reason why I even for a moment considered coming back to Pleasant Grove was because I didn't want to face the facts. I wanted to go on believing that what we saw and felt that night was as real for you as for me. But of course, I see now that I was a fool."

"I'm terribly sorry, truly — " she managed with tremulous lips, her eyes misted by tears.

Tom nodded, his haggard face stiff and grave. "Are you, dear? Thank you," he said evenly. He turned toward the door.

Megan said swiftly, "Will you come back to Pleasant Grove?"

He shook his head. "There's nothing to come back for now," he told her in that same quiet, almost toneless voice.

He was gone before she could

manage any sort of reply. She stood very still, until she heard the sound of his car dying away into silence. She ached with pity for him. She had never been so sorry for anyone in all her life; but there was a queer sense of lightness, too, a feeling almost of relief. She felt free of some old darkness, free and alive — and an individual, again herself, Megan MacTavish! She laughed again at the absurdity of such feeling as she ran upstairs to change for supper.

She was sorry for Tom Fallon; but for the first time, he was merely a friend for whom she grieved. And it did not seem possible that she had once thought herself wildly in love with him, so much in love with him that she had refused Laurence when he had asked her to marry him!

She could see now, in the sudden sharp clarity of her understanding, that Tom had had the lure of the unfamiliar. Aside from the fact that she had been roused to pity for him, he had been someone new and strange; while Laurence had been the familiar, the man she had known all her life. There had been no mystery, no surprises about Laurence. Perhaps she had even been a little bored with knowing him so well.

Well, that phase was over. She was just as sorry for Tom as she had ever been; but she knew now that she had never loved him and that she never would. By the very fact that he had, even for a moment, considered returning to Pleasant Grove and its tragic surroundings, she knew how bright had been the hope she had given him. And she could have wept for this new and bitter hurt he had met here.

Annie's voice, calling her to supper, tore her from the unpleasant groove of her thoughts and she went hurriedly down to find her father waiting, filled with the small, unimportant excitements of his day, and the job that he was enjoying so thoroughly.

As Annie passed about the dining

room, attending to their wants, Megan felt her eyes upon her, sharp and worried and anxious. Then she lifted her head and smiled at Annie and she could almost see the relieved sigh that Annie gave as she read and understood the look in Megan's eyes.

17

ON Sunday morning, a glorious June morning with the brilliant sun lying like a benediction on green fields and gardens burgeoning with roses and zinnias and marigolds, Megan went again to the Ridge.

She had avoided it all these weeks, pretending to herself that she was too busy, that there were tasks to be performed that made it impossible for her to make her favorite walk. But now she knew that she had lied; she had been afraid. And that was pretty silly, too — afraid of the old, beloved familiar scene, afraid of the giant trees through whose tops the eternal wind whispered softly, afraid of the view that gave her the green tops of fruit trees surrounding a shabby, drab little house of which now she could see only the tip of a fieldstone and dirt chimney.

She put her shoulders back and lifted her head, her eyes closed, sniffing deeply and gratefully the soft, faint summer wind that was rich with the scent of fields and woods and growing things.

The sudden sharp barking of Dixie warned her of the approach of some stranger. She turned sharply and looked across the meadow, and her heart stood up on tiptoe. She felt as though it, too, yelped with excitement. For even at this distance, she knew that figure. It was Laurence.

She sat very still and watched him, while a new, sweet warmth spread throughout her body. Her heart shook a little and her hands closed themselves tightly in her lap. The sunlight glinted on Laurence's bare head as he walked with his hands in his pockets, his shoulders drooping a little.

And watching him as he plodded up the meadow slope and across the fence, she knew a contentment so deep, so warm, so sweet, that she was one with the June scene all about her.

He looked up as the two dogs, recognizing him, raced to meet him.

And then he was close enough to see Megan, and he said with a little quick, meaningless smile, "Hello! Mind if I intrude?"

"You're not intruding — didn't the animals make that plain? We're all glad to see you," she told him, and smiled and patted the rock beside her, inviting him to sit down.

He threw a few pine cones for the dogs to chase, and when they had gone on about their business, he looked down at Megan and said quietly, "Annie thought I'd find you up here. Why did you want to see me?"

Megan's eyes widened a little and she asked, "Why did I want to see you? That's a funny question — "

Laurence frowned. "Well, after all, when Annie telephoned me — "

Megan gasped, and the hot color flowed into her face as she stammered, "Annie telephoned you?"

Laurence nodded. "She said you wanted to see me and that it was important, so I hitched a ride over. Why? What's the matter?"

Megan was scarlet. She could not quite meet his eyes.

"Annie — Annie had no right to do anything of the sort," she stammered.

Laurence's tired face hardened a little and his eyes were cool. "I take it, then, that Annie was mistaken in saying you wanted to see me — "

"I had nothing to do with the call," Megan cut in. "But of course, I always want to see you, Larry. Why wouldn't I? You are my oldest and best friend."

"Thanks a lot," said Laurence dryly. "But that's not good enough, Megan You know where I stand, where I've always stood, so far as you are concerned. I'm not fond of torturing myself, so I've kept away. I thought this morning when Annie telephoned me, that you were in some kind of jam, and that you needed me. And of course, that would always be the one thing that would bring me as fast as I could travel. But if Annie was wrong — "

"Look, Larry," said Megan huskily, "I've — well, there's something I have to tell you and it's not very pretty. I'm — ashamed — but you'll have to know it — "

"There's nothing I have to know about you, Meggie, that would be hard for you to tell me," he interrupted her swiftly, his eyes upon her, tired, somber, steady. "All I need to know is what you want of me. If it's possible, I'll do it."

Megan caught her breath on a sob and burst out swiftly, "Oh, Larry, don't be humble! I don't deserve it. I've been an awful fool — but now that I can see clearly — now that I know what it's all about, you make me so ashamed!"

Laurence stared at her, puzzled, a little resentful.

"Why should I make you ashamed, Megan? I think I resent that! You'd better explain," he said sharply.

Megan put out her hands in a little

gesture of pleading.

"That's what I'm trying to do, Larry," she told him unsteadily. "I'm trying to explain that I was fool enough to believe that I — was in love with Tom Fallon. And now I know that I wasn't — that I never was, really — " Her voice dissolved in tears and for a moment she hid her face in her hands and was very still.

Laurence stared at her, his brows drawn together. His hands made a little involuntary movement towards her but he stopped himself just before he could touch her.

He waited until she had herself under control and then he said, "And so?"

Megan lifted her face to him, childishly unaware of the tearstains, her whole being intent on revealing to him the secret truth locked deeply in her heart — locked so deeply that it had taken the shock of seeing Tom Fallon again to break the seal so that she herself could glimpse the truth.

"And so, when Tom Fallon came to

see me this week," she said with a forced steadiness, "and told me that he had been offered the school at Pleasant Grove again, and wanted to know whether I wanted him to take it — "

Laurence said quietly, when her voice broke again, "So he loves you that much? That he's willing to come back here to a place that must seem a little like purgatory to him — poor devil!" The last two words came in a breath of sound.

Megan nodded. "Poor devil!" she repeated and said huskily, "I'm so terribly ashamed, Larry — "

Still frowning, confused, Laurence repeated, "Ashamed, Meggie? Why, in heaven's name, should you be ashamed of the love of a man like Tom Fallon? I should think you'd be proud — "

"Ashamed because I let him believe that I — loved him," she said simply, her eyes on Laurence, watching him with an intensity that was almost a prayer.

For a long moment he was still, and then he said, "You let him believe that you loved him? You mean — you don't?"

She shook her head. "That's what I've been trying to tell you," she said unsteadily. "I — didn't know that I wasn't in love with him until that afternoon. I was so sorry for him and — well, I let my sympathy carry me away. I've been thinking I loved him, but when he came and stood in the living room, and looked at me and asked me whether he might come back to Pleasant Grove — and I knew what he meant — that if he came back, he would want me some day to marry him — I knew then that I couldn't *ever* — "

Laurence looked down at Megan and said evenly, "And what makes you so sure you never were in love with Fallon, Meggie?"

The deep, rich color poured into her face, but her eyes met his steadily. "Because I know now that — it's always been — you, Larry," she told him huskily.

For a moment he made a little convulsive movement as though he would sweep her into his arms. And then instead he stood up and walked away from her, and stood with his hands jammed into his pockets, his back to her.

Megan waited, the breath suspended within her. Had she waited too long? Had Laurence turned from her to someone else? Had he stopped wanting her? It would serve her right, to lose him — but if she had — oh, dear God, if she had — she put the knuckles of one clenched fist against her lips to hold back the cry of pain in her heart.

"*Larry!*" she whispered, and did not realize that the little sobbing breath had made a sound that had reached to him.

He turned sharply and came back and stood above her, his clenched hands still jammed into his trouser pockets, his forehead knotted, his face pale and set.

"You — you've changed, Larry? You — don't want me any more?" she whispered desolately. At that, he bent and swept her up into his arms and held her so close and hard against him that she could scarcely breathe.

"You know darned well I haven't changed, Meggie," he told her, his voice rough with emotion. "It's just that — can I be sure you're — that you know what you're doing? I'm no bargain, Meggie, matrimonially speaking. Hush, let me finish. I'm the slow, and plodding type; I'll never make a lot of money or be able to buy you fine things. You'll have to work — "

She flung back her head and laughed richly.

"Work? Oh, the very thought of work frightens me to death," she told him gaily, giddy with the relief from the fear that she had lost him. "You know *me* — I've never done a day's work in my life and I wouldn't know how — you blessed idiot! Are you trying to

212

frighten me? Well, you succeeded. You nearly scared me to death. Oh, Larry, Larry — don't — don't scare me like that again."

His arms tightened and he held her closely, his cheek against hers. "It's just that I lost you once, Meggie, and it — well, it just about finished me. I thought everything was fine between us and that we were going to be married, and then you kicked me out of my fool's paradise, by saying it was Fallon. I couldn't quite take it if you changed your mind again. It's got to be — well, final, this time, one way or the other."

There were tears in her eyes, as she stood on tiptoe and framed his face between her hands, and set her mouth on his, her warm, soft mouth that was faintly tremulous and very sweet and that flowered beneath his kiss.

"Oh, Larry — darling Larry — I do love you! I'll always love you. Forgive me?" she whispered unsteadily.

For answer, his arms tightened and his lips found and claimed her own.

WITH SOMEBODY ELSE
Theresa Charles

Rosamond sets off for Cornwall with Hugo to meet his family, blissfully unaware of the shocks in store for her.

A SUMMER FOR STRANGERS
Claire Hamilton

Because she had lost her job, her flat and she had no money, Tabitha agreed to pose as Adam's future wife although she believed the scheme to be deceitful and cruel.

VILLA OF SINGING WATER
Angela Petron

The disquieting incidents that occurred at the Vatican and the Colosseum did not trouble Jan at first, but then they became increasingly unpleasant and alarming.

DOCTOR NAPIER'S NURSE
Pauline Ash

When cousins Midge and Derry are entered as probationer nurses on the same day but at different hospitals they agree to exchange identities.

A GIRL LIKE JULIE
Louise Ellis

Caroline absolutely adored Hugh Barrington, but then Julie Crane came into their lives. Julie was the kind of girl who attracts men without even trying.

COUNTRY DOCTOR
Paula Lindsay

When Evan Richmond bought a practice in a remote country village he did not realise that a casual encounter would lead to the loss of his heart.

ENCORE
Helga Moray

Craig and Janet realise that their true happiness lies with each other, but it is only under traumatic circumstances that they can be reunited.

NICOLETTE
Ivy Preston

When Grant Alston came back into her life, Nicolette was faced with a dilemma. Should she follow the path of duty or the path of love?

THE GOLDEN PUMA
Margaret Way

Catherine's time was spent looking after her father's Queensland farm. But what life was there without David, who wasn't interested in her?

1	6/08	25		49		73	8/10
2		26		50	1/08	74	
3		27		51		75	
4		28		52		76	
5	10/13	29		53		77	
6		30	8/07	54		78	
7		31		55		79	
8		32		56		80	
9		33		57		81	
10		34		58		82	
11		35		59		83	
12		36		60		84	
13		37		61		85	
14	7/05	38		62		86	
15	11/12	39		63	12/15	87	
16		40		64		88	
17		41		65		89	
18	12/01	42		66		90	7/11
19	8/05	43		67		91	
20		44		68		92	
21		45		69		COMMUNITY SERVICES	
22		46	8/12	70			
23		47		71		NPT/111	
24		48		72			